A Salamander at Bell Station

and other tales

Beyond East of Eden

by

R.P. McCabe

Pen & Ink Publishing, Ltd.

Printed in the United States of America

Cover art and design: Yevinn Graphics

Edited by: G. J. Hedlind,
          University of California, Irvine

Also by R.P. McCabe

Betrayed

Thick Fog In Pacheco Pass

In memory of John Steinbeck
(1902 – 1968)

There was a time when the moon was my
friend. Its brightness crossed the night sky as a
constant reminder, that the distance between
us wasn't that far if you could see it too.
But now this very same moon mocks me
and follows me wherever I go.
It seems I can't hide from it at all
nor hide from the thought of you.
What once was my guiding light
has now become my stalker.
Its cruel glow will not allow me to fade
into the depths of dark despair.
It just laughs at me here
and you out there … somewhere.

… Poet, Brenda Sommer

Table of Contents

i

Introduction

John Steinbeck was one of the greatest American writers of the Twentieth Century and an American literary treasure. He was born in Salinas, California in 1902. The Salinas Valley, Monterey Bay and the Pacific Coast would become the backdrop for some of Steinbeck's greatest works.

Between 1919 and 1925 he occasionally enrolled in writing and literature courses at Stanford University but departed without any degree. Steinbeck would spend the next five years of his life as a laborer and journalist in New York City while working on his first novel, *Cup of Gold*, which was published in 1929.

Shortly thereafter, Steinbeck married and returned from the east coast to take up residence in Pacific Grove, California. In

1932 his novel, *The Pastures of Heaven* was published, followed in 1933 by *To a God Unknown* and *The Red Pony.*

Steinbeck continued to struggle financially until 1935 when his work began to gain popular success with his stories about Monterey's Italian Paisanos, *Tortilla Flat.*

During the 1930s Steinbeck began to focus on the laboring classes of the Salinas and San Joaquin Valleys; the itinerant farm laborers migrating out of the southern Great Plains, particularly Oklahoma because of the great drought, popularly called the Dust Bowl, and the Great Depression. His interest in this culture produced *In Dubious Battle* (1936), *Of mice and Men* (1937), a collection of short stories, *The Long Valley* (1938), and the novel some would call his finest work, *The Grapes of Wrath* (1939).

In 1941 Steinbeck tried his luck at filmmaking, writing the script for a documentary called, *The Forgotten Village.*

The film depicts the conflict between traditional life in a Mexican village and the outsiders who want to bring modernization. That same year Steinbeck became a serious student of marine biology joining his close friend and sometime muse, Ed Ricketts, in an ambitious voyage down the Pacific Coast of Baja California, around its southern cape, Cabo San Lucas, and up into the Sea of Cortez.

Steinbeck served as a war correspondent during WWII. His contributions to the war effort were, *Bombs Away* (1942), *Cannery Row* (1945), *The Wayward Bus* (1947), *Pearl Harbor* (1947) and *A Russian Journal* (1948).

In 1950 Steinbeck produced an experimental drama called, *Burning Bright.* The results of Ed Ricketts research during the famous voyage into the Sea of Cortez were released in 1951 with Steinbeck turning the log from their voyage into a narrative; *The Log From the Sea of Cortez.*

East of Eden, perhaps Steinbeck's most ambitious work, and my personal favorite, was published in September 1952. It is the saga of his own family's history in the Salinas Valley and lends considerable insight into Steinbeck's fascination with the Okie migration of the 1930s.

Steinbeck's later works included: *Sweet Thursday* (1954), *the Short Reign of Pippin IV: A Fabrication* (1957), *Once There Was a War* (1958), *The Winter of Our Discontent* (1961) and *Travels with Charlie in Search of America* (1966).

Steinbeck passed the last few decades of his life with his third wife, Elaine, between New York City and Sag Harbor. Posthumously, a number of Steinbeck writings have been published: *Journal of a Novel: The East of Eden Letters* (1969), *Viva Zapata!* (1975), *The Acts of King Arthur and His Noble Knights* (1976), and *Working Days: The*

Journals of The Grapes of Wrath (1989).

In 1940 John Steinbeck was awarded the Pulitzer Prize for fiction. In 1962 he received the Nobel Prize for Literature.

Photograph property of the Nobel Foundation
Used under Commons License
Photographer unknown

John Ernst Steinbeck Jr., born February 27, 1902 in Salinas, California, died December 20, 1968 of heart disease at the age of 66 in

New York City. Steinbeck was a lifetime smoker. On March 4th, 1969, John Steinbeck's cremated remains were interred in the Hamilton family gravesite in Salinas, California, alongside his mother, Olive. His third wife, Elaine, joined him there in 2004.

*   *   *

At the time of their deaths in 2001, neither of my parents would have had any idea who John Steinbeck was. And yet, they knew nearly all of Steinbeck's stories at least as well as he; for they were the stock of whom he wrote many of his great novels: *In Dubious Battle, The Grapes of Wrath, Of Mice and Men* and the stories of *The Long Valley.*

My parents were both children of the post-Depression pre-WWII south, whose families were steeped rich in poverty, were poorly educated, and had to scrape for every small opportunity that came their way: Dust Bowl

Okies. Steinbeck's rebuke of society in general for how the characters of his novel *Tortilla Flat* were regarded stands as a constant reminder to me of how a very large segment of American society regard cultures within our national community they don't understand or in relationship to whom they feel themselves somehow superior. In this, John Steinbeck and I are brothers. His illumination of their struggles changed for me, not just how I see people, but how I see myself.

My family arrived in the Salinas Valley well behind Steinbeck's. My grandfather, Willie McCabe, first made the trip from Ada, Oklahoma to Soledad, California in his 1927 Ford Model T pickup in the late 1930s, before WWII. My uncle, Willie McCabe Jr., was one of the first of the McCabe clan to migrate from Oklahoma after the war. My father followed shortly after him in 1947 when I was six months old.

The McCabes, a family of four girls and five boys (there was a sixth who died as a result of a head injury as a young boy), including husbands and wives, settled mostly in the Soledad area, but literally up and down the Salinas Valley from King City to Salinas itself. My father went on up to Salinas where an Army buddy promised him work. Another of the McCabe boys, Thomas, and his sister, Eddie, stopped in Taft, where Thomas, and Eddie's husband, found work in Southern California's oil fields. My grandfather and grandmother later migrated to the San Joaquin Valley and settled in Fresno, California where they lived out their lives. A large contingent of their brood still resides in Fresno. My father and mother migrated out of the Salinas Valley by way of Coalinga, California, finally arriving in the tiny San Joaquin Valley town of Gustine, where I graduated from high school.

My family roots remained firmly tied to the Salinas Valley. The richest memories of my youth are of our family trips up the windy ribbon of what was then called, 'blood alley' (California Hwy. 152) over Pacheco Pass to Salinas where the Friday and Saturday night get-togethers with family and friends often included singing, dancing, a few drunken pushing contests among the young men as though they were bandy roosters set to a cock fight, and wonderful feasts of barbecued chicken, potato salad ... sometimes homemade candied yams with marshmallows melted over the top. Memories of Bell Station, Casa de Fruta and Pacheco Pass, situated in Central California's Diablo Mountains near the southern limb of San Francisco Bay, tethering the Salinas Valley to the San Joaquin Valley, bind me forever to my childhood.

Digging deeper into childhood memories I still have gossamer visions of being pulled along dry dirt rows of mature cotton in a sea of white, literally being dragged behind, lying atop the cotton picking sack draped across my mother's shoulder. I could not have been more than three years old, but those images remain with me even today. My Uncle Willie called it *pulling bowls,* as he related stories of those times to me in later years. The entire family would descend to pick the crops.

I think I shall never forget the day it occurred to me to look up the word ignorant, only to learn it did not mean unintelligent or slow-witted. I began to think of my parents differently after that.

Serendipitously, one miserable cold winter evening in the early seventies, newly discharged from the Army, I was living in Denver, Colorado. The wind was howling, snow whipping about. I flipped on my television to find the original black & white 1940 movie, *The Grapes of Wrath* about to begin. I'd never read the novel or seen the movie. I became uncomfortable as Henry Fonda, Jane Darwell, John Carradine and O.Z. Whitehead began to play out a story I knew all too well. It felt awkwardly personal. I knew those people. Well … I knew people who could have been those people. The earliest memories of my childhood had been painfully close to what I was seeing. I knew who John Steinbeck was, but I'd never read one of his novels. That changed on that evening in 1972, and I have felt an uncommon bond with Steinbeck all of my adult life. I was stunned when I first saw a photograph of John Steinbeck. He and my father looked enough alike to have been related. And it would only be later, after I'd read *Of Mice and Men,* that I experienced another startling revelation, as my father's nickname was Curley.

You might imagine my astonishment when I learned I'd grown up nearly in Steinbeck's shadow, literally next door to where the great writer once lived. I might have brushed past him one day, or sat eating fish & chips with my father in one of the restaurants on Fisherman's Wharf at a table near his, 1955 perhaps. I was just a boy of eight years. Steinbeck may have moved on by then, I'm not sure. *East of Eden* was written in 1952.

My Aunt Lilly Pearl lived in a small cottage in Pacific Grove, across the street from where the famous aquarium now stands, not far from where Steinbeck himself once lived. At that time, many of the closed up relics of sardine canning buildings still stood as a reminder of a time forever gone; as nearly extinct as the sardines themselves. I'd play there among the tumbledown buildings of burnished bricks and broken windows with my cousins and other kids from the neighborhood, completely oblivious to the backdrop of Steinbeck's great novel, *Cannery Row*.

In 1984 I paid private homage to Steinbeck when I sailed my Alajuela cutter, Arabesque, from Newport Beach, California down and around the horn of Baja California and up into the Sea of Cortez. It was a journey filled with mystery and promise, for I had purchased and read Steinbeck's, *Log from the Sea of Cortez*. The *Log from the Sea of Cortez* was literally the ship's log from the ambitious journey made by Steinbeck and Ed Ricketts for the scientific cataloging of invertebrates for a textbook destined to become required reading in most college courses where the study of marine biology was the curriculum. The text was written by Steinbeck's best friend, Ed Ricketts, and called *Between Pacific Tides*. At the time, I was merely interested in traveling in Steinbeck's wake. I determined to use *The Log* as my navigation guide, retracing every port-of-call and visiting the tide pools and remote villages described in the book.

One of my most romantic stops up in the Sea of Cortez was at a small lagoon called Amortajada (A slice of love.) There was a small village nearby. A relic of an old man remembered a wooden trawler bearing two young *gringos* anchoring in his lagoon forty-odd years in his past. He recalled as a boy spending hours wading with them through tide pools while they collected specimens. A painful grimace clouded the old man's face, as if something significant in his life had been taken from him when I told him Ed Ricketts had been killed in a horrible accident when his car was hit on a railroad crossing just a few years after returning from his Sea of Cortez adventure. Ed Ricketts was the character, Doc, in Steinbeck's famous novel, *Cannery Row*.

I chose the title to Steinbeck's epic novel, *East of Eden*, for this tribute, aside from the fact that the writing is one of the finest examples of literary prose ever written, because it is the saga of his own family's history in the Salinas Valley. My family history is also deeply rooted in the Salinas Valley. John Steinbeck's work inspires in me a belief that who I am as a man ... a writer ... is enough.

> *"I always found in myself a dread of west and a love of east. Where I ever got such an idea I cannot say, unless it could be that morning came over the peaks of the Gabilans and the night drifted back from the ridges of the Santa Lucias."*
>
> ... John Steinbeck – East of Eden

Okie's Boys

THE VISCOUS BLOWS landing sounded like two flat pieces of wood being slammed together. Thwack! Andy screamed. Whack! Andy peed all over himself. He was trying desperately to protect himself from the brutal blows of daddy's wide, rough-studded leather belt.

"I'll break ye from suckin' eggs ye little bastard," daddy bawled.

I dove from my bunk to the floor and made a run for it when I heard the old man tear back the blankets on my brother's bed. Sneak attack was one of the old man's favorite tactics. I was always alert to the possibility; especially if I figured Andy and me might have it coming, like that morning.

*   *   *

When daddy, climbed behind the steering wheel of his tired `52 Chevy to go to work that morning, the straight-block six-cylinder engine was still warm. Andy and I'd left only a quarter tank of gas in the tank daddy'd filled the night before. To make matters worse, we'd forgot the pair of white nylon underpants we'd swiped from a clothesline on the front seat. Didn't take a genius to figure out we'd pushed the old car down the driveway and a ways up the street after he'd gone to bed and then run off prowling through the night.

It would take years for me to understand the full extent of the financial hardship stunts like that caused my father and why his rage could have been so manic. All I considered at the time was he was a mean son-of-a-bitch and damned hard to escape when he was pissed off.

It was just sun up. Daddy was

supposed to be on his way to work. Easy enough at that hour to catch us sound asleep. Pure luck-of-the-draw he hadn't gotten at me first that morning. Of late it seemed to work out more often than not, Andy was first in line for daddy's irate rages. Still, the old man was never too spent to whoop me, too. Good Southern Baptist folk like momma and daddy held a solid *ass-whoopin'* was what the Lord ordered for disobedient boys, which was exactly what us two "little bastards", as daddy was given to calling my brother and me, were.

I worked my way around behind the old man while he was busy with Andy. I was helpless to do anything about it except to piss him off even worse and get the hell whooped out myself for my failed effort.

Out on the rickety back porch of our tiny house I shivered in the cold morning air wearing only my threadbare undershorts. They hung baggy around my skinny legs and sported a sizable tear along one leg working its way around to my fleshless ass.

I knew full well if the old man came out this way I'd get the same as Andy, for sure. Naked as I was, there was nowhere left to run.

Finally, I heard daddy and momma yelling at each other, then the violent slam of the front door. It was rare for momma to take daddy on, but on those occasions when he went too far, like that morning, she'd finally step in to call a halt to his doings. I exhaled a nervous sigh. In a few seconds the old Chevy cranked up and pulled out of the driveway; the crackling of small stones under the weight of the wheels signaled the old man was really driving away.

For several more anxious moments I crouched, trembling, my hands cupped together, held up over my mouth. A warm vapor of breath escaped along the sides of my face as if I was trying to stanch a drag off a cig. An eerie silence settled in over our tiny four-room house. The stagnant smell of scorched Andouille sausage from last night's supper still hung in the kitchen. I could make out the muffled sounds of Andy's sobs coming in heaving, snot-sucking gulps. The gas burner in the hot water heater swooshed alive and the sound of water running through pipes replaced the mean after-noises of the morning's appalling beginning. Momma was running a warm bath for Andy.

There wasn't much new in the chaos of what occurred that morning. The question in my head was, how bad did Andy get it this time?

I crept slowly across the cold, worn linoleum floor of the kitchen toward the open bathroom door. There I found momma kneeling over the side of the bathtub, drizzling warm water over the welts crisscrossing Andy's back and legs. The water began to turn a sickening shade of pinkish-brown; some of the strikes were so harsh they actually cut Andy's skin.

"You okay, Andy?"

"Yeah ... I ... I ... guess so."

Momma verily whispered her words. "Damn it, Cotton. What did you boys do this—"

"Nothin', momma." I tried to cut her off … maybe change the course of what I figured was coming. "I swear! We just sneaked the car out for—"

"Gotdamnit, Cotton," she shouted, standing. I knew when momma took the name of the Lord she was really mad. "What you mean, nothin'? You know damn well sneakin' your daddy's car out ain't just, nothin'." She was shaking. "Look at what you boys went and made your daddy do." Momma made a face of disgust when she studied, Andy's back. "Nothin'," she stammered, seemingly talking to herself. And then she sprang at me. "Gotdamnit, Cotton! You're thirteen years old! You know better! Now, look!" She pointed to Andy's wounds once more. "Just look at your little brother's back." Momma did this with the clear intent that what I saw was my doing, my fault. Andy was a year younger than me. He was scrawny but wiry; he could be like a lizard crossing a hot rock in the summer sun. His ribs showed under the oozing welts over his back as he bent forward holding his close-shaved head in his hands.

"Wadn't Cotton's fault, momma." No matter the circumstance, Andy always rose to my defense. "It was my idea. Cotton didn't even wanna go."

Momma ignored him. "Why you boys gotta go off 'n do such like this? You know your daddy's gonna' catch you." And then her voice softened slightly. "And you know what he's gonna' do to you. And yet you go right on ahead. Y'all don't learn." She rinsed the washcloth in the bloodstained bath water. "Go on … get yourselves ready for school."

Momma stood and straightened her worn, flimsy nightdress. She looked weary trudging toward the kitchen to start breakfast.

"Let me put something on those cuts before you put your shirt on," she said over her shoulder.

"Okay, momma." Andy said. "I'm sorry … I didn't mean to make daddy mad. Really, I didn't." Andy carried a load of guilt, which was a trait momma tended to impart owing to her belief in the word of the Lord toward how children were supposed to look upon their parents, and the obligation of their parents to administer harsh penalties for wickedness aimed at keeping a disobedient boy on the Righteous path. No matter our willingness to repeat offenses against our parents, Andy was convinced they had an obligation to straighten us up, because that was what the Lord required of them. And we, as the offenders, were required to accept our punishment with humility. I'm not so sure how to gnaw on that, "Ya'll don't' learn," part. Andy and me pretty much always seemed to take the left fork in the road when we should've gone right. Momma was never successful at selling me that snake oil story about what the Lord required of her and daddy or the load of guilt attached to it, but she had Andy convinced.

I didn't say anything—just stared darkly into my mother's eyes. If hatred described what I felt for daddy that morning, contempt was the dose of medicine I reserved for momma. She was always on his side. She'd watch him whoop us, or if it suited her purpose she'd incite him to it and then blame us for making him ireful, as though what he did to us was somehow justified, and always our own fault; we had it coming.

Andy and I shuffled off to school in silence. We alternated kicking an empty Pabst can that happened into our path.

"What're ya gonna' tell yer gym teacher, Andy?"

"Old man Watson don't notice shit. I'll keep my shirt on. He won't see ... I done it before."

A train belched and whistled some distance up the tracks. We searched to find it.

Andy thought for a minute. "I fell on a bob-wore fence?" He waited to see if I thought that would be convincing.

"Yeah. I mean … I guess so. Probly work." I was pissed off over the lies Andy and I would end up telling to explain our afflictions. "How come you always apologize to momma when that son-of-a-bitch whoops you?"

"Ain't her fault, Cotton." Andy was quick defending momma, too.

"She damn shore don't do nothin' to make 'im stop, neither."

"What's she s'posed to do? Lord says daddy ain't got no choice but to lay wood to us. 'Sides, daddy's big. Anyways … makes her cry." He paused thoughtfully. "I figure me sayin' I'm sorry might make her feel some better."

27

My resentment toward both daddy and momma grew. But it was clear Andy saw things different. He'd get pissed off at the old man all right … even momma sometimes. But he never stayed mad at either one of them long, and he bought momma's story about what the Good Lord required of her and daddy.

"I'm gonna' knock `im on `is ass someday." The words squeezed out of me as I let fly an empty bottle I'd snatched up along the way.

"You better not let daddy hear you say somethin' like that."

"Don't worry, when I'm big enough," the bottle exploded against the railroad track, "I'm just gonna' do it … ain't gonna' bother tellin' `im first." We laughed uneasy, searching the depths of each other's souls: Andy to see if I meant what I said, me for any sign he might betray me to our father.

It was seven o'clock and dark by the time daddy pulled the Chevy into the driveway. Supper was waiting. Nobody was allowed to eat until daddy got in. Didn't matter how late that might be or how hungry we were.

I watched him wash up at the sink. Momma ordered Andy and me to do likewise.

Andy'd already had his whoopin' so he came running in hungry, ready to eat. He'd already shoved the morning into his forgotten past.

I waited out on the porch. If daddy had it in mind to give me a whoopin', he was going have to catch me first. I'd learned if I could avoid an intended belting long enough, daddy could get distracted and forget he hadn't taught me the Lord's lesson.

"Get on in here 'n eat yer supper, boy." Daddy pulled his chair back and sat down heavily. "I'm 'onna' whup yer ass later."

I edged my way into our tiny kitchen.

Wouldn't be the first time the old man lied to get close enough to catch me. I had no appetite, but I took my place at the table like I was told. But I never took my eyes off him; he made one wrong move, I was ready to get.

The Saturday before, daddy had Andy and me out in the fruit orchards gathering mustard greens that'd been planted under the trees to keep the weeds down. Most people didn't even know you could eat that stuff, but momma and daddy could come up with more ways to fix those things than could be imagined. Momma set a pot of the boiled greens, rice and pinto beans on the table. It wasn't fancy, but there was plenty.

An uneasy quiet settled over our oily little kitchen. The only sounds were the scraping of the spoon against the rice pot and heavy exhalation noises escaping daddy's nostrils while he gnashed.

"You boys wonna tell ye momma what ye done last night?" Daddy didn't bother looking up from his plate. His voice was calm but menacing.

Andy and I were confused: old man losing his marbles, maybe? Momma already knew what we did last night. Momma and daddy exchanged a glance.

"Nooo!" Daddy sang the word mocking us. "I guess I wouldn't want my momma knowin' neither, I had some little ole gal out all night." Daddy's Adam's apple ricocheted up and down while he took a long swig of beer, "'N took her panties off 'n left 'em on the front seat of my momma's car.

"What else you boys do to that little gal on that front seat?" Daddy slammed his beer bottle down hard on the metal table. "Ye wonna tell ye momma who it was you boys was puttin' the prod to last night? Ye wonna tell ye momma 'bout that?" I could see daddy was gleeful at having created just the right mental image to draw momma into the fray.

Momma's brown doe-eyes grew

enormous, magnified even bigger behind the lenses of her heavy framed glasses. She raised her head slowly and eyed me … Andy … back to me. "Cotton—? Andrew—? What-have-you-boys-done?" She pronounced each word as if it was a separate sentence.

I protested the false accusation. "We didn't have no little ole gal out all night, momma. Honest we didn't."

"Don't you boys lie at ye momma like that," daddy threatened. "I'll knock ye teeth plum down ye th'oats."

Andy took daddy on. That was one of the reasons daddy whooped Andy before coming after me, some kind of payback that evened the score to daddy's low way of thinking.

"Honest, daddy. We didn't have no gal out last night." He looked the old man in the eye. "We swiped them underpants off of Elle Vernon's clothesline. We was just gonna' tease her 'bout it later on … honest, daddy. That's all we done."

I decided to brave the denial once more but purposely addressed momma with my rebuttal. "That's the truth, momma. That's how we got them underpants."

"We're sorry, momma," Andy followed up, turning to face her.

There he went again. Apologizing to momma for something daddy started.

"Well," momma growled, "you boys are gonna' take them underpants straight over to the Vernon's house and give `em back to Elle Vernon in front of her parents."

"Yeah! `N then I'm `onna' whoop hell out o' ye again."

"Been enough whoopin' around here today." Momma let her fork tumble noisily onto her plate. "You boys get this table cleaned up. Gonna' drive ya'll to the Vernon's house myself." Momma raised herself slowly out of her chair. "And if you ever pull another stunt like this," she regarded Andy and then me, "I'm gonna' whoop ya'll when your daddy's done witcha!" Apparently the Lord had spoken on the subject and she'd received His instructions direct.

That was the closest momma ever came to defending us from daddy's abuse— promising to join him in delivering the next round of punishment seemed to keep her on his side, which was damn well where she'd better be or she might find herself getting the same as us, as happened from time to time. I suppose the Lord directed momma on those matters as well.

*　　*　　*

"You boys get ye fishin' poles. Let's see cain't we get us a mess o' catfish."

On Saturdays, if daddy didn't have some legitimate excuse for getting away from the house, he'd concoct something to do with Andy and me. Fishing was one of his safest schemes. He could be sure momma wouldn't want to come along. Andy and I would provide the proof we'd actually gone fishing with what we'd catch. And we knew damn well to keep our mouths shut about where we actually ended up.

"Let's go fishin'." That meant we were headed for Catfish Camp down on the Merced River. The hangout was a bait'n tackle-beer-bar-meet-up joint sure to have a couple of floozies lurking about mooching for somebody to stand them a few beers.

One of daddy's favorite pastimes was telling bullshit stories, lies mostly, drinking beer and sniffing around loose women who hung out in the back rooms of the trashy dives he drug Andy and me around to. The Lord apparently spoke to daddy different than he spoke to momma.

Daddy'd guzzle Lucky Lager and play grab-ass with those women all afternoon while Andy and me did the fishing. If it got hot, sometimes he'd buy us a Coke or a Shirley Temple, Seven-Up with a little Maraschino Cherry juice.

The only beer money my old man ever had was the few bucks he scrounged from scabbing side jobs now and again. He had to be careful because if his boss, Axle Harper, ever found out, he'd fire daddy for sure. Daddy couldn't afford to be buying beers for his *lady* friends. That's why he had to settle for feeling them up, I expect.

Somehow daddy managed to come up with pocket money most weeks. Then he was stuck coming up with a plan to get out of the house without momma tagging along.

It had to be without momma because the things momma could put her foot down about and get away with were beer drinking and woman chasing; devout Baptist woman. Momma was good at suffering her burden. When it came to anything else in our lives, daddy made, and enforced, the rules. Nobody better gotdamn well interfere with what he wanted, neither; at least that's how the Lord speaks on the matter of a husband and father's rights according to daddy. And daddy was always a good follower of the word of the Lord just like momma.

On the way out to Catfish Camp, daddy doled out his usual orders. "Stay out the damn store 'n keep ye mouths shut when we get back home."

Once daddy needed our cooperation to cover his ass, I knew Andy and I could relax some until the next time we pissed him off. Of course, where daddy was concerned, Andy and me could never be too careful … or sure of ourselves. Divine intervention could fall upon daddy without notice, and nothing would do but a solid ass-whoopin' in the interest of obedience to him or the Lord; I was never quite sure which.

Of the places daddy hung out, Catfish Camp was okay by me. It was a mile or more down a dirty, narrow road lined with rushes of cattails and massive clumps of blackberry brambles, scraggly cottonwoods and willows whose branches held powdery dust like a fresh snowfall strewn with the paper packaging from fishhooks, worm cups or hamburger wrappers and empty beer cans along the river's banks. The river could get shitty in flood season. Andy damn near drowned swimming across it once while it was running wild with muddy water and downed trees and the odd dead cow after days of heavy rain. Andy was always taking chances like that.

The store was a ramshackle two-room wooden shanty with a raised front stoop that looked like the swayed back of an old plow mule. Looked more like a barn: wood weatherworn and gray from old age and neglect. The roof on the end closest to the river sagged a little, as if it just might slide off into the water. Broken down outboard motors and rotted wood boats were propped like logs on a beaver dam against the dilapidated outside walls. A lopsided black sign hanging over the front door with curled grimy white letters scrawled across it divulged where you were: Catfish Camp.

When Andy and I were little, a thick hemp rope hung from a branch of the gnarled live oak shading the side of the building closest to the river. There was a truck tire tied to it we could swing on. Gone now, like the happy memories I held to playing on it. Anyway, we were too old by then for that kind of kid's stuff.

Daddy bought us Cokes right off that day. Andy and me baited up with big juicy bloody-looking night crawlers and hung a couple red and white bobbers on our lines to float the fat wigglers just off the bottom. We settled at the shady end of the drooping porch and put out our poles. Every now and again peals of laughter reached us from inside the shack.

"You think daddy ever fucks them ole gals, Andy?"

"Got the money, I bet he would. Shit, I wouldn't mind gettin' on ole Stella myself. She ain't that ugly 'n she's kinda young." Andy looked toward the front door as he heard another lusty squeal. "You see them tits o' her's when we pulled up?"

What Andy said left me feeling scratchy. I couldn't explain that then. A feeling, after all, just is. There was a lot beginning to trouble me about that time in my life.

Andy's escapades bordered on criminal, and he became more and more like daddy each year. Both of them were generously steeped in the word of the Lord but with interpretive variations that would challenge the best of any good churchgoer. He hardened, too, and became more fearless with every new whoopin' daddy dished out. He rarely cried anymore when daddy whooped us. Guess he figured if he could survive that, what the hell could anybody else do to hurt him?

We were finishing our Cokes when a dented rusty-red, spot-primed Ford pickup skidded to a dusty stop in front of the store. Two unshaved, mean-faced roughnecks climbed out. I recognized them as the two mechanics from Axle Harper's garage, where daddy worked.

"Ain't them Okie's boys?" one of them said as he mounted the stoop.

They pulled the door open to the dark bar and yelled, "Hey, Pussy!" just before slamming it closed.

Andy shrugged. "Daddy ain't gonna' like that." Daddy's name is Percy.

We lazed a good hour on the grassy riverbank chewing dandelion stalks. We'd caught six catfish apiece. Fishing had lost its appeal.

Suddenly the door of the shack busted open and daddy stumbled out backward and off the porch. "Ye sons-a-bitches," he yelled. "I told ye not to call me that." He shook his fist at the grubby menace in the doorway.

"Yeah, 'n I tol you, Pussy, you ain't nothin' but a fuckin' white trash Okie. 'N if'n you don't like it, you kin jest try doin' somethin' about it." The greasy, whisker-faced thug mocked daddy leaning against the doorjamb.

Stella half stumbled out onto the porch holding a Lucky Lager. "You gonna' let `im cuss at ya that-a-way, Percy?" she slurred.

Daddy didn't answer. By then all six occupants from the bar'd poured out onto the stoop like a pack of coyotes about to tear a rabbit apart. Daddy just stared at them all looking down on him.

It was a big game to them, daddy's tormentors, Stella, the other old barfly ... all of them. If there was nobody else around, daddy was acceptable. But as soon as anybody else came along, daddy ended up being picked on and made fun of. I'd witnessed these scenes many times. I was beginning to form the opinion daddy brought a good deal of this trouble on himself, though there seemed to be other forces I didn't yet understand at work, too.

No one noticed Andy and me come up onto the side of the splintered porch until we were already standing right alongside Stella. Suddenly, everybody stopped yelling and stared at us as if this was grown-up business, not suited to be carried on in front of a couple of snot-nosed boys.

The static air between the ugly participants was charged with menace like the low, groaning rumble just before a bolt of lightning snaps. Everybody waited to see who would make the first move. My skinny twelve-year-old brother took four deliberate steps and stopped in front of the bully standing in the doorway.

He looked up at the man and said, "Yer name's Levi, ain't it?" Andy's tiny voice was controlled, not a quaver.

"That's right, boy! You know me?" Levi eyed my little brother contemptuously.

"Know who you are," Andy said, completely relaxed. "Yer the asshole that jest called my daddy a white trash Okie." Andy pointed his reedy index finger at the brute. There was coldness in his voice that sent a shiver up my spine.

Levi laughed loud, called to his buddy. "Hey, Frank ... you hear this little shit call me an asshole?"

Stella joined in, giggling uproariously at Andy's insult. Suddenly, Andy hauled off and kicked Levi square in the balls as hard as he could. The thug screamed and grabbed his crotch, bending over in agony. Andy swung his empty Coke bottle hard upward, landing it across the bridge of Levi's nose. Squishing cartilage made a sickening noise. Blood squirted out of Levi's nostrils and the gash now in the middle of his face. The blood running everywhere was so dark it seemed almost black to me.

"That little bastard broke my nose," Levi wailed, going down on his knees.

Andy began screaming in Levi's face. "Ain't nobody gonna' ever talk to my daddy like that, you son-of-a-bitch!"

Levi's partner lunged for Andy

through the door, but I threw my bottle at him and charged. I managed to knock him off balance before he reached Andy.

Daddy dove for the tire iron under the front seat of the old Chevy, but Lucky the bartender'd seen enough. He grabbed his blackjack.

Lucky growled through clenched teeth glistening with gold and brown tobacco stains. "That's enough, boys." His voice was ominous with the message that somebody was going to end up in the hospital or jail or both if they went against him. "Load up." He pointed to each of the participants with his weapon. "All o' ya get your asses out o' here ... NOW!

"Levi," he rasped, "you ain't welcome here no more."

It got so quiet I could hear the gurgling of the river from where I stood.

*   *   *

The ride back to town seemed to go

on forever. Daddy drove deliberately slow, smoking Pall Mall after Pall Mall, tossing them one after another out the car window, sparks flying as they hit the pavement. Daddy studied the rear view mirror like he expected to find something there, or maybe it was just a nervous twitch. I can't say. He was in deep consideration of something. I felt sure Andy and me were in big trouble again.

About five miles from town daddy pulled the car off the road and got out to take a leak. When he went around to the passenger door and opened it, I figured that was it. The Lord must have spoken, and Andy and me were going to get the shit whooped out of us. Daddy says to Andy, "Come on out o' there, boy."

I held my breath. There wasn't going to be much we could do way off out here alongside an open road. The old man watched as Andy slid slow-like out of the car. He looked up at daddy preparing to protect himself.

"You wonna drive?" There was the slightest trace of gentleness in daddy's voice as though he was prickly or embarrassed speaking the words in that tone. His face did not bare what his true thoughts may have run to. Daddy was like that, never able to express his feelings with words.

Once in a while after he'd whoop the piss out of us, I'd see daddy go off by himself outside and weep. It took me all the way into adulthood and a long way down that road to begin to grasp the complexity of who my old man was and why he did such things as he did. And yes, by then I'd knocked him on his ass without any prior notice. But not that day.

"Thanks, daddy!" Andy's face broke into a grin that spread like piss across a mud fence. He raced around the rear of the car to the driver's side and slipped behind the steering wheel. He could just see through its upper arc.

I tasted vomit rise into my throat.

Suddenly, I needed to take a leak, too.

A Salamander at Bell Station

Plastic Soldiers

THE BULLET RIPPING INTO MY FLESH felt warm, almost friendly. Had the concussion blast from a mortar round not crushed my eardrums and numbed my senses, I might not have thought my wounds more than an inconvenience.

Life and everything connected to it was receding in slow motion. I lay dying in a shallow depression excavated by a bustling colony of cutter ants. The industrious Atta cephalotes seemed less perturbed by my presence than excited at the prospect of a new meal. The ants began eating me. They started with the sweet blood oozing from the gaping hole in my side before carving some better cuts of meat from the soft tissue around my eyes.

Better than what happened to Smitty two days ago, I suppose. The rotting tree he crawled up to during the firefight was the nest of a protective cobra and her freshly laid eggs. Her fangs caught him in the corner of his left eye. Smitty stumbled to his feet screaming, the grotesque yellow serpent hung on, pumping her venom deep into his brain.

The gooks did him a favor cutting him in half.

I registered the putrid smell of napalm-charred human flesh and faint cries seeming to invade from a world beyond the one I was about to leave.

*　　*　　*

"Haul you ass out dat bed, T Jean. Tink you gonna lay up half the day jest 'acuz it's a Saderdy? They's work to get done, boy. Damn well better not still be a waitin' when I get home."

Frenchie wasn't my real father, but he

was the only one I ever knew. Momma took up with him down in Baton Rouge after the war, and I been stuck with him ever since.

"He gone yet, momma?"

"He gone. Better go on get up and get your chores done you wanna go out 'n play."

I relaxed into my pillow, breathed deep, sucking down the cool morning air, redolent with the smell of onions ready to be harvested. Frenchie would have threatened to beat hell outta me for that.

The first time he did hit me, momma threatened to kill him if he ever touched me again. Frenchie must have believed her because he only pushes me around or kicks me in the ass. He never actually beats me, just threatens he's going to.

Momma can be unpredictable. She might just take a notion to give me a good whippin', but she usually lets me get away with a few extra minutes lying in of a morning.

I loved the time of year, the end of summer, early autumn, air crisp in the mornings, crops being harvested everywhere from King City to Gilroy. The air outside smelled like one of momma's gumbos, boiling `atop her stove. The zoom … zoom Doppler sounds of a distant crop duster wafted through my open window along with golden rays of morning glow. I pulled myself outta bed and bent to my chores.

How we came to settle in the Salinas Valley I can't really say. I was but six months old when Frenchie put momma and me on the train at Lake Charles, Louisiana and sent us out to California. That would have been 1945. Frenchie followed with all of his and momma's possessions folded into his 1936 Buick. He arrived ten days behind momma and me.

Frenchie didn't know anybody out in California. He was just out of the Army after the war. Couple of Army buddies he served with wrote him they thought he could find work there. Frenchie did find work with

Ocean Mist Farms. They grew artichokes.
Frenchie didn't know anything about
artichokes or any other crop for that matter.
Before the war he poached alligators and ran
moonshine down on the Bayou Fourche in
southwestern Louisiana. But he drove a
deuce-and-a-half during the war, and that
was enough to land him a tractor-driving
job. Momma said it was the best pay
Frenchie ever had, and for that we were able
to live like real white folk.

Both momma and Frenchie were
always concerned that they be considered
regular white folk as so many people who
worked the fields of Salinas Valley,
regardless the color of their skin, were not
considered so. As I grew to become an adult
during the 1950s, I observed more and more
the intricacies of the ethnic system we live
under in America despite the boisterous
claims of freedom and equality, fellowship
and patriotism.

Equality, it seemed to me, traversed
from the top down. It depended on whether

or not your ethnic group controlled where you lived and worked and just how high up the scale that group was in the broader sense of the American quilt. People who picked crops alongside Mexicans in the Salinas Valley were white all right. But it simply meant they were the white in white trash. What was so important to momma and Frenchie was that with Frenchie's job, we weren't 'pickers'. And that made us, as momma held, like real white folk. Seeing as how we were elevated to the status of real white folk, it fell to Frenchie to see that we held our station in life and didn't go socializing with niggers, Mexicans or Jews.

I didn't know what a Jew was, much less the significance of socializing with them, until I met Roland Finkelstein. Roland was the only Jewish kid in our school, and I never actually learned how his mother came to settle in the Salinas Valley seeing as how they seemed so isolated from other Jews. It was hard to find a Jew in Salinas in those days.

Frenchie constantly lamented that the damn Japs and Chinks and Jews were invading San Francisco and Salinas, too. Frenchie held that they were much lower forms of life than the Paisanos or Ports, as he referred to the Italians and Portuguese, which was all to elaborate the notion that since we were not pickers, we were somehow elevated to a class above those classes and only slightly demoted to a standing below that of full fledged white ... whatever the hell that meant. Frenchie and momma could be hard to follow on this point.

By nine o'clock I was down the road knocking on the door at Roland Finklestein's house. "Hi, Mrs. Finklestein. Rollie come out and play?"

Roland remained a secret friend. I was careful to slip away from my house in the opposite direction from where the Finklesteins lived, and then double back through the fields to the south and down the road to Roland's house. Whether momma ever knew, I can't say. If she did, she never gave me up to Fenchie, and she never interfered with my friendship with Roland Finklestein.

"Hi, T Jean." Mrs. Finklestein often answered the door in her panties and brassiere. She had a big black bush that was escaping the sides of the crotch of her white panties that was hard for me to take my eyes off of. I'd come to regard the sheer swampyness of her crop with some trepidation as recently I'd noticed a patch of growth taking place just along the top of my pecker. The contemplation of achieving something on the magnitude of Mrs. Finklestein around my own crotch was somewhat disconcerting. "Roland!" she shouted kindly, smiling down at me, "T Jean's here. He'll be right out, T Jean."

Mrs. Finkelstein stood silently, smiling down at me studying her bush for several moments but did not invite me in. She never invited me in. She was younger than momma and pretty, with dark eyes that seemed almost black. A mane of thick curly black hair cascaded onto the tops of her titties. She was pretty, all right; pretty and sad, you ask me. Mrs. Finklestein was always nice to me, though. "What are you two boys up to today?"

"Playin' soldiers, mamm."

"Best be careful with that rock throwing."

"Hey, T Jean." Roland Finklestein appeared from behind his mother's wide hips swinging a red pale by its handle.

"Hey, Rollie."

"Remember what I said, boys. Watch the rock throwing."

"Sure, ma." Rollie squeezed past her.

We marched to the edge of the irrigation ditch about a quarter mile from Rollie's house. A big black car rolled past and honked its horn as it pulled into the Finklestein's driveway. The guy that got out and went inside was a field boss. I didn't know who he was. It was just the way he walked; the way he glanced contemptuously toward Rollie and me—field boss right enough.

The ditch had been used to irrigate the fifty acres of tomatoes raised in the field next to it. Mexicans'd already picked them clean, and the field was plowed under by then. The ditch was dry with hard clods of clay dirt, ideal for stacking and throwing. We built two forts about ten yards apart and two foxholes to defend our territory.

"Green or brown?" Rollie demanded while he separated the plastic soldiers in his red bucket.

"Can I be green this time, Rollie?" I studied how fat Roland Finklestein actually was while he contemplated my plea. Kids at school called him, Rollo Finklestein, the fat assed Jew; called me the elephant-eared Cajun. We both felt defective. I think that's why we spent so much time together. We didn't seem to have anything else in common—except we liked playing war with Rollie's plastic soldiers.

"You know Lebeau, green's my favorite—geh`head, you're gonna lose anyway." A grin rolled across Rollie's face like white powdery sugar off a doughnut.

"I gotta pee, Rollie. How 'bout you?"

"Yeah, me too."

Kneeling in the ditch we unzipped and began tracing circles in the dry dirt.

I'd been noticing the difference in how our peckers looked for a long time. That day I asked Rollie about his.

"Circumcised," he explained, looking down at his pecker. "Jewish boys get it done the eighth day after we're born. Called our *Brit Milah*. Family all gets together and reads a bunch of prayers from the *Siddur*, eats a lot of food and then cuts the skin off our peckers. Kid squeals like a puppy gettin' its tail whacked off. They don't do it to girls." Rollie and I ogled each other momentarily thinking that last observation over. "Ma takes me to Synagogue and family stuff when we go up to San Francisco. I seen it done. Why mine looks like a pickle and yours looks like the blow up end of a balloon," Rollie said, pointing at my pecker.

"You think your daddy loved you, Rollie?" Roland pondered the question a few moments.

"I guess so. I mean, he sent me letters clear from Korea 'n all. Ma says before he got killed he wanted me to be a doctor just like him. You ready?"

I unleashed a rain of dirt clods aimed mostly at Rollie's plastic soldiers, but several found his foxhole. He rapid-fired back until truce was called.

Scorekeeping was exacting. A soldier had to be knocked completely down or be buried under a dirt clod to count as dead. As usual, after we counted up our kills, Rollie won. He picked bigger clods than me to throw.

I was sure being green would bring me luck. It hadn't.

"Wanna play again next Saturday?" Rollie offered.

"If Frenchie has to work. You know what he says 'bout me playin' with niggers or Jews. If he ain't workin', I can't sneak off."

"See ya, T Jean." Rollie waddled back toward his house. The big black car was just pulling away.

*   *   *

"Medic! Medic! Lebeau's hit, man! Perdy bad, sarge!" Salazar was crying and pissing his pants while he stuffed bandages from his field pack into the softball-sized hole in my side and brushed the biting ants from my face.

A Huey hovered just off the ground in

a small clearing seventy-five yards away. Two scared soldiers helped PFC Tony Salazar drag my limp body across the open ground while Vietcong popped shots at them getting me out.

After that, I ceased to exist until eternity came full circle and decided to acknowledge my presence in the oblivion of its vacuum.

"T Jean?" The voice coming to me was from far away, yet gentle, vaguely familiar.

I'm dead, I thought. Was that God's voice? I'd often wondered if we had any memory of life after we died. I had no sense of being. I was nothingness, and yet my mind seemed to toil as it had when I was alive. I was confused, but certain now; in death, I really was going to be plagued by every bad deed I'd ever committed. Maybe there really was going to be a hell—heaven, I suppose, if you were a better person than me. Maybe God was coming to talk to me now, to judge me, punish me maybe. I could try asking him to forgive me the bad deeds I'd done in life—worth a try.

"T Jean, can you hear me? T Jean?"

I wanted to answer but I could not.

"Doctor Finklestein, they need you in the OR, stat!"

"Right there, Hattie.

"T Jean, it's Roland Finklestein. Can you hear me, T Jean? You're going to make it. You hear me ... T Jean? You hear me? You win! This time ... you win."

The Summer of Elvis

ONE HOT, WILTED SATURDAY AFTERNOON in early September 1956 Earl Larson, Jack Grayson and me, Ed Dawson, stole two cases of empty pop bottles from behind Stuggie's corner grocery. And it wasn't the first time we'd pulled that caper. We sold them back to the grumpy old man for the deposit, three cents each. Old man Stuggie stood pondering us from head to toe. Finally, he parted with the dollar and forty-four cents. Years later I learned Mr. Stuggie was completely aware of our occasional crimes against him. He always gave us the money anyway. I'm pretty sure it was not his intention to encourage our criminal activities.

That day we took our loot down to the Rexall and bought two malts. We drew straws to see who would get one of the cold ice cream drinks all to himself. Earl Larson won. Had it been Jack Grayson, I'd have figured the draw was rigged.

We were sitting in a sticky, humid corner booth under the noisy swamp cooler flipping through the jukebox selections and scheming over our next heist when Earl says, just as casual as you please, "You boys wanna sleep over tomorrow night and see Elvis on the Ed Sullivan Show?"

Earl's father was a big shot at Contadina Foods up in Salinas. The Larsons were top of the heap in Soledad, owned one of the few television sets in town. The biggest event in the universe that summer would be Elvis Presley's live appearance on the Ed Sullivan show, but in Soledad, California, where we lived, not many kids would get to see him. Soledad was just one of the scrubby backwaters up and down the Salinas Valley where families like mine could survive between harvest seasons; or, in the case of Soledad, do your time up at the State Pen. Most of the permanent townsfolk were real churchgoers and didn't abide the nigger music Presley was trying to pawn off on their kids. *Picker* families like mine were too damn poor to own a television set.

I guess I looked on the place harsh as I did because my life was altogether different from Earl's and Jack's. My family was pickers: cotton, lettuce, tomatoes—you call it. When the season was on, that's what we did, all of us, me included.

My uncle, Chester Dawson, was over in the prison doing eighteen months. Knocked a field boss on his ass for shoving his pregnant wife while they were picking cotton. Chester beat his face in for him. Big bosses and the cops didn't abide pickers or hobos getting uppity. Any of us got too far outta line, and they'd all be on us hard. That was my life, lot different from Earl or Jack. Jack's folks had education. They worked at the City Hall.

My father said if I had any hankering

for education, I could have all of it I wanted, 'right after we're done pickin'.

"That would be so cool, man." Jack pronounced the words like he was a real beatnik. Jack had an older sister, Kat, who lived up in Frisco in the North Beach. Each time he returned from visiting her, there was a new layer of 'the scene' attached to him. Jack was one of the vanguards of the Cultural Revolution taking place in the big city and therefore one of the coolest cats in Soledad.

"You really think your parents would let us?" The invitation sounded too good to be true to me.

"Already asked `em," Earl revealed, drawing a big sip through his straw. "Whataya think?"

Jack used the distraction to suck the last of my share of our malt out of the glass. Then he kept making loud slurping sounds wearing a cocky smirk on his face. Jack's skinny neck and beak-shaped nose reminded me of a turkey. I don't think he ever understood how lucky he was I didn't alter the shape of that beak of his.

You really think we could?" I was more interested in Earl's offer than the loss of the malt.

"Only us three. Momma warned me." He stopped a moment to swirl his drink. "What about your folks?"

Jack answered for me. "Ed's old man's a real asshole. He'll have to get permission first." My father did have the reputation of wearing a chip on his shoulder. I think mostly it was frustration over his lot in life and his inability to claw his way above it. He couldn't abide Jack's smart mouth and *cool cat* ways. He'd run him off from the house when Jack would smart-mouth. Jack considered he was doing me a favor even being friends with a picker's kid.

I stared Jack down for the remark and the malt. "I'll have to ask," I was forced to admit. "Pretty sure I can."

"I don't even need to ask," Jack bragged, gawking at me. The words curled off of his thin lips in a snarl. I was never more than a friend of convenience to Jack Grayson. And how friendly he was toward me depended solely on who he happened to be with when he ran into me.

The soda jerk behind the counter shouted over to us to take a hike unless we were going to order something else.

Jack shouted back. "Fuck you, man," and we ran for it. The guy ran out to the sidewalk in front of the place, hands on his hips yelling after us, watching us run up the street.

"What the hell'd you say that for?" shouted Earl, his chest heaving.

"Don't sweat it, man." Jack's arms pumped faster than ours. "He's nothin' but a fag."

We made it to the corner and around before slowing down to make sure the soda jerk hadn't decided to come after us.

"Jesus, Jack." Earl was bent over, his chubby hands clutching at his throat, gasping for breath. "Now we can't go back in there when that guy's working."

"He's a fag, man." Jack's sweaty face was contorted. "He's gettin' fired 'cause of it. Buddy o' mine works there; told me so. We ain't got nothin' to worry about. Just be cool, man."

This was another bit of wisdom Jack was importing from San Francisco of late. There was a pretty big neighborhood of queers and such moving into San Francisco and starting to attract attention. *Cool cats,* like Jack and his buddies, were out to do somethin' about that. If Jack decided he didn't like somebody, he started calling him a fag. That was the word he used for queer, and he and his other buddies were known to give a fag a good working over from time to time for no better reason than they decided that's what a fag deserved.

One weekend back in June, Jack went off to San Francisco with his folks to see his sister Kat. When he caught up to Earl and me on his return, he was sporting a swelled up eye and bruises up side his head. "We was workin' this queer into an ally to teach him a lesson," Jack explained. "Me `n my two buddies offered `im five bucks to suck our dicks. When we got back down between some buildings the fag says, 'money first.' So we pretend like we're getting it out. That's when the sumbitch says, 'Two things I like to do boys—fight `n fuck.' Fucker jumped us plain as day. Nothin' but a damn trap. Next time I'm in the city, gonna get some boys, see can't we look that queer up—teach `im a lesson."

We spent the rest of the day at the City Park hanging around the public swimming pool. We made catcalls at the girls and performed other disgusting adolescent acts of disobedience until we were finally chased away by the lifeguard who threatened to call the cops. We retreated making loud fart sounds with our hands in our armpits.

By the time I'd finished my chores the following day and made it back to Earl's house, Jack was already there. His folks never asked much of him.

Jack and I gave Mrs. Larson our word we had permission to spend the night with Earl. After that, we made plans for seeing Elvis Presley live on the television. The possibility of that was about as exciting as anything that had happened in our young lives to that point and particularly that summer.

The house Earl's parents owned sat near the edge of a huge acreage of farmland on one side and the main street of town on the other. In the side yard was a pump house with a small loft. The building originally protected the well that irrigated the crops. It'd been converted to a storage shed. The Larsons painted it a soft yellow with white trim to match the main house. Two ancient, drooping willows dangled their reedy branches between the pump house and the back door to the kitchen. The Larson's house was one of the nicest in Soledad and, to my way of thinking, one of the handsomest.

Earl's father'd cleared out the black widow spiders and rats from the loft and turned it into a clubhouse. Wooden vegetable crates served as tables and benches. Earl even kept an old Army cot in one corner and was permitted to sleep up there sometimes. Earl talked his mother into letting the three of us turn the loft into a barracks Sunday night and sleep up there after the Elvis show.

We were staking out our territories when Earl says, "Hey, I almost forgot to tell you boys, seen my buddy Lloyd from Gilroy last night."

Jack spun and flopped onto his bedroll. "Bet there's tons of shit to do in Gilroy."

"Lot more'n here," Earl allowed. He pulled a crate over and perched his overweight bulk. "Wait'l you hear what him and his girlfriend done. You ain't gonna believe it."

I was as anxious as Jack for Earl to get on with the telling. I scooted over closer to him.

"Okay," Earl began, "I told you boys she's been lettin' him feel her up, right? Well, last week, she lets him give her a finger job, and she really liked it."

"You gotta be shittin'." Jack and me gasped the words almost simultaneously. I rubbed my sweaty palms on my pant leg.

"No, shit. And just wait'l you hear what else."

We squeezed in closer.

"Well, Lloyd's old man and old lady decide to go out of town while his brother's home from—"

A creaking sound came from the wooden stairs as if someone might be coming up. We all three sat up straight and tense, staring silently at the open doorway like three prairie dog pups. Turned out, just the bones of the old pump house complaining.

Jack was at Earl again. "Come on, come on, man. Get to the good part."

"Be cool, man." Earl had recently taken to using Jack's *beat* way of talking; that's what they called it, *beat*.

"So, anyway," Earl was saying, "Lloyd's brother goes off partyin' and leaves him home alone."

"Come on, what'd he do?"

Earl grinned; his head bobbed up and down ... baited us before going on with the tale. "So he gets his girl over to his house. They're completely alone. And he gets her up to his room." He stopped again, playing us like a couple of carp after a wad of soggy

Velveeta.

"Come on, man," Jack complained, rubbing his groin. A pained grimace crossed his face like November clouds off the Pacific. "I'm gettin' a boner just waiting to hear this."

Earl let the pause hang.

"She let him dry hump her until he shot it, man." Earl sat up straight, satisfied with his delivery.

My mouth felt dry. "You mean … they really did it?" I whispered.

"Not for real … Jesus. They kept their clothes on. But after Lloyd was done, she let him give her another finger job." Earl's buddy Lloyd was eighteen and, through Earl, fed every adolescent fantasy our roaring hormones could handle. All three of us would start high school at the end of the summer.

Jack jumped to his feet holding his crotch. "Man, that makes me wanna jack off."

"Me, too," I agreed. I was learning to be a follower if I wanted to get included in things. Earl and Jack, not being picker's kids, could go and do things I never could've on my own. All three of us had big bulges in our pants.

We were jumping around the loft, making phony faces, clutching at our boners as if we were in some kind of high grave pain.

"Hey, you guys ever done a circle jerk?" It was Earl's idea.

"Sure, man," bragged Jack. "You ever done a circle jerk with a chick watchin'?" Jack Grayson was not the type to be outdone.

I didn't want them knowing I'd never participated in any kind of circle jerk, observed or otherwise. "You gotta be shittin' me … with a girl watchin'?"

"Hey, I'm serious, man … with a

chick watchin'." Jack stabbed his lanky index finger in the air toward Earl and me to make his point.

Earl goaded him. "I think you're full o' shit, man." Earl was like that, clever, kind of. He was a lot smarter than Jack.

"Bullshit I am, man." Jack dragged the word *bull* out like it contained ten '*L-s*'.

Earl stroked Jack some more. "So who was this chick?"

"Raydawn Morgan," Jack claimed, gawking at us, allowing the image time to form in our minds.

Jack's reply was emphatic, but I sensed he wasn't telling the entire truth of it. Wasn't that I was so smart; just I'd been around Jack Grayson enough to doubt just about everything he said. Besides, I'd known Raydawn Morgan since third grade. She was in my third grade homeroom. She was a tomboy, as good at running and climbing and baseball as any of us.

Jack was acting like he had something to prove. "Know what I'm gonna do?" He answered his own question. "I'm gonna get her over here this afternoon, and we're gonna have a circle jerk while she watches."

When I think back on all of this, I really believe Jack Grayson was the only one of us who actually intended going through with his plan. Earl and me just didn't want to look like chicken shits. Neither of us expected Jack would even try to pull it off; things just wouldn't work out, and we'd all pretend to be disappointed.

After Jack took off, Earl and me conned Mrs. Larson into peanut butter and jelly sandwiches before heading off to the swimming pool. It was way too soon to try another caper at Stuggie's corner grocery.

The lifeguard managed to ignore our fart sounds and fake burps that day. Soon enough we were bored. Nobody was paying any attention to us. We finally drifted listlessly back to Earl's.

It was coming toward late afternoon by then. The only thing on my mind was seeing Elvis Presley on the television. Mrs. Larson said the show didn't start until seven o'clock. That meant we'd have plenty of time for the promised hotdog roast outside to be all cleaned up before the show came on. I realize now Mrs. Larson was nearly as excited as we were about seeing Elvis that night.

It looked like Jack still hadn't shown up by the time we got back to Earl's. Jack had a whole other set of friends that me and Earl never hung around with. They smoked cigarettes and cussed right out in the open and carried switchblade knives, always on the lookout for Pachucos lately. We figured he'd gone off with them.

While we waited to cross the road, Jack stuck his head out of the pump house door holding that scrawny finger of his to his lips. We ran across and huddled with him.

Earl cuffed him on the shoulder. "Where the hell you been, man?"

"You still in for tonight?" I asked Jack this hoping the answer would be no.

He had a cocky, fox-that-ate-the-chicken, grin on his face. "You boys got short memories." Jack was full of himself. "You forget what we planned?" He pointed up toward the loft.

Realization hit Earl and me like cow shit fertilizer on a wet field.

Earl's eyes widened. "You mean you got her over here?"

Jack affected a hurt look. "Bet your ass I did. Told you I would. Look, here's the thing. I didn't exactly tell her what we got planned. She thinks I'm cool, so let me do the talkin' and don't do nothin' to scare her. Got it?" He turned and sprung cat-like up the stairwell.

Earl seemed eager to follow. I fell in and went right along with them.

I was last into the loft. Raydawn was standing on the opposite side of the tiny room staring suspiciously at the three of us. I could tell she was scared. That was the very first time I'd noticed anything more about Raydawn Morgan than that she existed. Standing there eyeing her, it occurred to me she didn't wear pigtails anymore. Her silky blond hair'd been bobbed to just above her shoulders. The way it was parted down the middle, it accented the soft curve of her smooth forehead. Her eyes were large and brown and sparkly and set off, in a most appealing way, the gentle sprinkle of freckles that flushed faintly across the bridge of her nose. Her eyebrows were full, and a peach flush of color glowed against her olive cheeks, but she wasn't rouged with pencils. She had on a short blue dress, tied high at her midriff. And she had grown a lot taller.

She tossed her head sideways nervously and brushed her hair back. "What are these guys doing here, Jack? Thought you wanted to make out a while."

"Well ... I do." Jack's voice sounded mousy, and it squeaked on the end of what he was saying. "I didn't know they was gonna be back so soon. Kinda surprised me. Know what I mean?"

Raydawn actually appeared to accept the lie.

"So, can we go someplace else?" she said, biting her lower lip.

Jack moved awkwardly around a wooden crate toward her, shoving his hands deep into his pockets. "Well, it's kinda like this, Ray." He fidgeted and looked back over his shoulder toward the two of us then back to her. "The guys here, well, they sorta had a little party planned this afternoon 'cause we're all gonna get to watch Elvis on the television tonight."

It didn't matter to Jack Grayson that Raydawn's folks didn't have a television, that Ray would have wanted to see Elvis just as much as any of us. Ray's folks were pickers, like mine.

Raydawn went rigid. "What kind of party?"

Jack put his arm around her shoulder. "It was just gonna be the guys, but now that you're here, they asked me if you wanna stay?"

Raydawn looked as cold and stiff as an ice cycle. "What kind of party?" she repeated, enunciating each word slowly.

Jack had a half-cocked grin on his face. "Circle jerk," he announced smart-ass.

At that Earl started to giggle.

"And you want me to watch, just like the last time, right? And if I refuse, you're gonna tell everybody I did anyway. Then you're never gonna come around to see me again, right?"

Jack shrugged his shoulders. "I never said nothin' to nobody about the last time, did I?"

There was a sickening silence in the loft for several moments before Raydawn dropped her eyes to the floor. "You guys have to hurry," she said in a whispery voice. "I have to get home."

At Jack's coaching we formed what amounted to a semi-circle about five feet in front of her. Jack and Earl unzipped their pants and started jacking off. I stood there as if a load of shit'd been poured over me. Seemed like only a matter of seconds before they were finished, but I hadn't even managed to get a boner.

Earl and Jack stared at me in disgust. I was humiliated. I couldn't do it, and each passing moment made the situation worse.

Earl tried to encourage me. "Come on, man. Hurry up."

No use. I was pathetic, barely able to keep from crying.

"What the fuck's the matter with you,

man?" Jack demanded.

Raydawn raised her eyes from the floor to meet mine. She hadn't actually watched any of the ridiculous performance.

Jack went on reviling me. It was obvious he was enjoying himself.

"Hey, man. Leave him alone," Earl finally said.

Raydawn gazed deep into my eyes for several moments. Then she stepped over and took my hand. "Come on," she said softly.

She turned and glowered at Jack Grayson. For several seconds no one moved, and the cocky grin faded from Jack's face.

Raydawn's soft hand in mine was like touching fire that didn't burn. She led me down the stairs, across the road and up the street. She held my hand gently but firmly and said not a word. After a few paces we stopped and turned to look to the window in Earl's loft. Jack and Earl looked down at us but made no gesture and yelled nothing at us.

Raydawn held onto my hand. "Let's go," she said. We turned back up the street walking slowly toward Stuggie's.

When we got there, I realized she had huge tears in her eyes. "I gotta go home," she said, loosening her grip, letting my hand fall free. She regarded me for the longest time but said nothing.

I never saw Elvis Presley on the Ed Sullivan Show.

*   *   *

Earl, Jack, and me didn't see much of each other by the end of that school year. We just drifted apart, each seeming to grow in a direction that didn't include the others. It wasn't purposeful or intentional, I don't think, although what happened that day remained a burden between the three of us. We were about the business of becoming the people we were destined to be.

Our high school years validated the

subtle drift that began that summer of Elvis, and by the time we'd graduated, none of us even remembered or admitted that we'd once been friends.

Raydawn Morgan once told a girl I dated she thought I was a nice boy. I've always wondered if that was an indictment or forgiveness.

A Salamander at Bell Station

The Man in the Tool Shed

TRAVIS MALLOY stretched his spare eight-year-old frame up onto his tiptoes to reach the battered straw basket he'd hung from the sagging barn door the previous night. The weary dwelling his parents rented on the outskirts of Gonzales, California spared enough room around it to keep a milk cow, Earline, whom they would eat if she stopped giving up her juice, and a pig Travis named Carmelita after a girl at school for whom he felt the pig bore a strong resemblance, and two dozen scrawny russet-red hens indentured to Harry Truman, the nastiest gimpy-legged bandy rooster outside the state of Oklahoma.

The red hens would lay their eggs in different places every few days. Travis had studied their furtive habits and established a decided advantage over the witless birds ...

as long as he steered clear of Harry Truman.

He pushed aside the door to the tool shed expecting to find one of the bony hens sitting on the burlap bags in the corner. Instead, he came face to face with a frightened pair of wide-set eyes that seemed unnaturally huge, so big they appeared popped out of the head they belonged in.

"Who ... who are you?" Travis stammered.

"Damn, boy! You like to scared life out o' me sneakin' up like that."

"How'd you get in there?"

"Don't be afeared, boy. It's jest me, ole Curry. I ain't gonna' hurts ya." The man reached out with an up-turned palm that was several shades lighter than the rest of him.

"What're you doin' in there?" Travis demanded once more. "Daddy catches you, he'll whup yer ass, sure."

"Don't `spect so, son. Believe was yo' pappy brought me yere `n gimme this ole place to sleep in." Curry dropped his hand to his side.

In the open space of the barnyard,

Travis found his courage, curiosity mostly. He eased back toward the doorway, and inspected the stranger from the top of his natty head with its halo of dust down to the rotted brown leather shreds attached to his feet.

"How come daddy to bring you here?"

"Yo' pappy stopped aside the road `n axed me what was I doin' hitchin' up in these yere parts. When I tol' `im, said he might have a few chores I could hep wif 'round da old place in exchange fer a place to sleep `n some eats." Curry squinted at Travis. "`Spect you be lookin' fer eggs, boy." He nodded toward the crumpled bags in the corner.

"How you know that?"

"Cuz you got you a basket fo' eggs, `n that ole red hen flew outta yere when I come in was sittin' on two fresh laid ones."

"Travis, supper's on." It was his mother's voice. "Come get washed." Travis's eyes shifted toward the house.

"Best get on up to ya house, boy." Curry handed Travis the two warm eggs.

"What'd you say was your name?"

"Most folks jest calls me Curry-the-nigger."

Travis chewed on that a moment.

"That make you some mad, mister?"

Curry studied Travis's inquisitive eyes. "Best get on up to ya supper, boy. Yo' momma gonna' come lookin' fer ya."

* * *

The aroma of hot, sweet cornbread saturated the tiny kitchen. Travis squeezed up next to his brother, Jonas, at the sink.

"There's a man in the tool shed," he whispered.

"Blow bubbles out yer butt!" Jonas shouted, elbowing Travis's shoulder.

"Jonas Malloy, you watch your mouth, boy. Your daddy'll tan your hide he hears you cussin' like that," snapped the boys' mother.

"Really, Jonas," Travis insisted. Dirty soapsuds swirled down the drain.

Travis took his seat at the table and scooped out a chunk of cornbread and smothered it with three spoons full of pink beans before topping the concoction off with a dollop of raw honey.

"Get ye some o' them turnip greens, boy," his father growled.

"Aw, da—"

"Shet up 'n do like I tol' ye, boy." Paddy Malloy glared threateningly at his son.

Travis didn't argue, and he took the smallest serving he thought he could get away with.

Spoons clinked against plates. Other than the occupational sounds of food being gnashed, the cozy kitchen was quiet.

Without warning, Paddy's voice boomed out like a radio turned on with the volume set too loud. "You boys keep away from that tool shed. They's a nigger boy a stayin' in that shed. Y'all keep clear of it, y'ear?" He shoveled a spoon full of beans and turnip greens into his mouth.

Travis knee-butted Jonas under the table and mouthed, "Told you." Then he turned to his father. "I already run into 'im, daddy," he confessed. "Name's, Curry."

"Niggers ain't got names, boy … 'cept

`mongst they own." Paddy gave the boy an evil glare over the top of his beer bottle.

"But he told me—"

"Yon't me to slap yer mouth, boy? I told you, niggers ain't got names. Back-talk me again, yer gonna' be eatin' four knuckles with that there supper. Stay away from that black devil. No tellin' what he might do he gets half a chance."

Travis chewed cautiously through the rest of his supper. An uneasy silence filled the anxious spaces between the sounds of food being gobbled.

"When you boys are done clearin' the table, y'all slop that hog good. I want her fat afore we slaughter." Then Charlotte Malloy turned to her husband. "Hon', you want me to make a plate for that ole nigger boy?"

Paddy'd just stuffed a piece of cornbread into his mouth. Crumbs shot out when he yelled, "Hell no! That nigger ain't done nothin' get no supper yet."

"But, hon'—" Charlotte stopped herself as Paddy erupted.

"I said no, 'n I mean no! The hell's wrong with y'all tonight? Ain't gonna' be satisfied 'till somebody gets they ass into it." He pushed away from the table and threw his fork. Beans and cornbread flew. He grabbed his beer and kneed his chair out of the way. "I'm 'onna listen to the fights 'n I better not hear one damn word outta them boys o' yers or you."

Travis and his mother kept extra quiet while his father tuned the radio to listen to the Wednesday Night Fights.

"You'll look sharp … and you'll feel sharp, too—" Travis sang along softly with the Gillette Cavalcade of Sports while he collected dirty plates and glasses.

He scraped leftovers into the slop bucket and stacked the dishes. Jonas ignored his mother's orders and curled himself up on the floor beside his father. Neither Travis nor his mother would risk complaining about it. His mother washed, and he dried before going out to feed Carmelita.

It was late spring, and the earth hoarded the warmth of the afternoon sun long into the cooling evenings. Up and down the Salinas Valley crickets fiddled, heralding the coming of summer.

Every acre of arable land between the Gabilans and the Santa Lucias had been planted, and the fusty odor of fresh-tilled earth filled the night air. It was an honest smell Travis loved. There was no moon in the inky-black sky, but he could still make out the brooding outline of the Santa Lucias to the west and the Gabilans to the east. The only sounds besides the crickets were muted voices coming from Paddy Malloy's radio, rising in excitement … and snorty oinks drifting on the night from Carmelita's pen. The dim glow of a nude light bulb dangling over the back door of the house attracted thousands of fluttering insects.

Travis didn't see Curry leaning against the tool shed as he shuffled toward Carmelita's pen. "Nice night it turnin' into." Curry's voice floated out of the darkness like a spotlight startling the boy.

"Who's there?" Travis searched for the voice.

"Jes me, ole Curry," he said walking out of the shadows toward Travis.

"Daddy told me I had to keep away from you."

Travis darted toward the pigpen.

Curry allowed some distance but tagged along. "That there slop fer ya pig?" he asked, pointing at the galvanized pail.

"Yep," Travis said. "Momma wants Carmelita good `n fat before we slaughter her."

They walked slower. Travis twice glanced toward the house. Carmelita oinked louder.

At the trough, Travis prepared to add some feed-corn and water to the slop bucket.

"What was it you said you called your pig?" Curry asked, hoisting a foot onto the bottom rung of the fence.

"Carmelita," Travis repeated.

"S'pose Carmelita there would mind if I was to jes taste a little o' her supper 'fore you mix in that there corn?" Curry waggled a long, reedy finger at the bucket.

"You hungry, mister?"

"Ain't et in more'n a day."

It was too dark to make out what was in the bucket. Curry used two fingers to fish around, taste what it was. "Greens," he announced. "Greens is good. Good fer ya, too." He tilted back his natty head and dangled several greasy strands into his mouth like a mother bird dangling a worm into the mouth of its young.

"Turnip greens," Travis confirmed. "I hate 'em."

"What else you got in yere, boy?" There was urgency in Curry's investigations as he dug deeper into the bucket.

"Rice `n beans," Travis reported, watching Curry scoop up another taste.

Without explanation, Travis handed the bucket to Curry and ran off toward the house. In a minute he was back with two pieces of cornbread.

"Here, mister," he whispered. "Try some of this."

"What you got there, son?"

"Momma's cornbread," Travis said with pride. "Go ahead, try it." He watched

Curry gobble, anticipating praise that never came.

Curry alternated between frenzied bites of cornbread and scoops of unidentifiable glop. When he'd finished, he looked down into the slop bucket and proclaimed, "Look like to me plenty left fer Carmelita." Travis agreed. Curry helped Travis mix in the feed-corn and water. Curry slopped the food into the trough for Travis.

They leaned against the fence listening to Carmelita rooting; edging herself closer to a destiny she wasn't much likely to appreciate.

Licking his fingers, Curry asked, "What be yo' name, boy?"

"Travis," Travis answered grabbing the top rail of the fence, pulling himself up. He kept an ear trained on the drone of the radio in the distance. If Paddy came out and caught him talking to Curry, he'd get the beating of his life, maybe Curry, too.

"Daddy says niggers don't have names, 'cept 'mongst they own." The declaration came out of nowhere, without malice of intent; rather, a deepening suspicion of things told to Travis by his father.

"Lot o' white folk feels that way," Curry allowed. "But my momma gimme that name ... Curry. Figger that make my name Curry."

Travis pondered the logic in Curry's assertion.

"See them stars yonder?" Curry pointed to a spot in the eastern sky above the Gabilans. "That what they calls O-rion. And them little bitty stars off there, why, them be the Li'l Sistus." Curry spoke softly, gently, but with an affirmation of wisdom. "I seen `em from the deck of a boat onct. Ain't nothin' perddier'n stars out over a ocean." He tilted his head back and gazed up into the dark, star-clustered heavens for several moments.

"Curry?" Travis, it seemed, was grappling with nagging hunches. "You hate white people?"

"That be somethin' you don't need to be worryin' `bout, boy." Curry turned, leaned his back against the fence.

"You hate me, Curry?"

"Why you worried 'bout sich things, boy?" Curry turned, scraped grease from his hands onto the fence.

"Lot o' folks don't like my daddy. Some kids at school don't like me neither. Call us white trash Okies, bunch of 'em do." Travis paused, arched his body to balance himself on the fence and let his feet dangle back and forth.

The statement lay there like a rotten tomato dropped from the vine.

"That seem to be the way o' most places I ever been, boy." Curry paused, as if to choose his words. "Somebody always thinkin' he better'n you. Don't pay no mind to it, son. You figger it out fo' yo' sef soon 'nough."

"You been all over the world, Curry?" Travis's voice brightened.

"Seen a lot of it," Curry claimed.

"What's it like, livin' on a boat?"

"Hard work. Hard livin'… but good livin'. You ever heared o' place called Trinidad?" Curry leaned down and pulled at his pant leg.

"Nope," Travis admitted. He shifted to take the weight off of his numb butt and raised himself a bit onto both hands.

"Down off the coast o' Souf `merica." Curry explained. "There durin' Mardi Gras onct. You ain't never heared the likes o' music `n dancin' `n singin'. Go on fo' a whole week. Night `n day. Don't never stop. Most perddiest girls you ever did see `n more food'n a man kin eat.

"Yes sur, Mister Travis. They be some mighty fine places in this yere old world." He smiled and patted Travis's knee.

"I seen a really big farm once," Travis announced, not to be outdone. "Daddy and momma took us to King City. When we was drivin', we went by this great big ol' farm by Soledad. Must o' been about a bunch o' acres or somethin'." He threw his arms wide. "Went all the way from the road up onto the foothills of the Santa Lucias. And they was long rows o' tall eucalyptus trees swayin' in the wind on both sides o' them fields … went back to them hills, too." He paused and looked down at his feet. "I'm `onna get me a place just like that someday, great big ole place." He shrugged, wiped his hands on his overalls.

It was silent again for a minute before Curry began winding down their dangerous reunion. He'd experienced the likes of white men like Paddy Malloy before.

"Man got to dream, Mista Travis. You'll figger that out fo' yo' sef, too, soon `nough." Curry touched him on the shoulder this time.

Carmelita had finished her supper. She looked up at Travis and made several breathy snorts.

"Best be gittin' back up to yo' house, boy, `fo they come lookin' fer ya." Curry pushed himself away from the fence and reached down to grab a handful of dirt, which he rubbed into his palms before wiping them both down the front of his shirt.

"Guess so," Travis agreed. "Maybe I'll see ya again tomorrow?"

"Maybe … maybe, boy." Curry headed toward the tool shed without looking back.

Travis reached the back door of the house just as his mother stuck her head out.

"Where you been, Travis Malloy? I thought you was in your room all this time. You got any studies to tend to?" She spoke to him through the rickety screen door.

"No, mamm."

"Go on, get yourself ready for bed then."

His mother opened the door for him and strained a glance across the dark yard.

*   *   *

It felt like the middle of the night to Travis when the lights began coming on in the house. It was still dark outside, but a grayish smudge had begun to show in the eastern sky silhouetting the Gabilans.

Travis struggled upright in his bed rubbing his eyes. He heard loud, angry voices and singled out his mother's.

"What's wrong, hon'?" she pleaded.

The screen door slammed in the background.

"That gotdamn nigger went'n run off durin' the night. I knowed it. No tellin' what he stolt. Get me my shotgun. I'm `onna find his black ass an teach `im not to steal from Paddy Malloy."

"Hon', don't go doin' nothin' like that."

"Gotdamnit, woman. I ain't got time to listen to yer carrin' on. He's gettin' away while you out here whinin'."

Travis recognized the familiar sound of shotgun shells being jammed into an open breach.

He listened while the frenzied scene continued to unfold. He and Jonas crept, side by side, into the kitchen in their baggy underwear. The smooth planks of the worn wood floor felt cold on Travis's bare feet.

"Y'all keep yer asses in the house," Paddy Malloy yelled.

Paddy went off in a rage into the darkness. Travis could hear the `44 Ford pickup complain against the grinding of the starter before it coughed to life. Rocks banged against the side of the house as his father spun the truck out of the yard fishtailing it down the lane.

"Where's Daddy goin' with the shotgun, Momma?"

"Don't worry about your daddy. He knows what he's doin'." Travis could see his mother didn't believe that. "Go on. Get cleaned up and I'll make y'all some breakfast."

Travis had just rubbed pomade into the stubbles of hair on his head when he heard the wheels of the old pick up grind to a stop outside.

His father kicked the garbage can out of his way when he returned the still loaded shotgun to its corner. "Black bastard got clean away. Must o' run off early last night." Paddy addressed this to no one in particular. "No trace of `im `round town or out at the highway. Now I got to figger out what that black devil stolt." Paddy paced back and forth ignoring all of them.

"You want some eggs, hon'?"

"Call me when they ready. I'm `onna have a look in the tool shed." The screen door slammed before Charlotte Malloy could get up from the table.

Travis and Jonas nibbled while their mother fried more bacon and eggs. The scorched bread was just coming out of the oven when his father came back in.

Paddy sat down without acknowledging any of them and crammed a whole chunk of thick, fatty bacon into his mostly toothless mouth.

Travis's mother chewed staring into her plate. "Look like he made off with anything, hon'?" she asked cautiously.

"Black devil got off with near ten pound o' them walnuts you was savin'." Paddy took a long, sucking sip of hot coffee.

Curry's words from the night before played in Travis's head. "Man got to dream, Mista Travis. Man got to dream—"

Travis closed his eyes as he swallowed a big gulp of Earline's cold milk.

A Salamander at Bell Station

WHEN I LOOK BACK ON IT NOW, I think it was tenderness I yearned for then. I'm reasonably certain of that. One lugubrious Thursday morning in the evanescent days of the summer that my father landed the best job he'd ever had and General Dwight D. Eisenhower was running for President, he packed our entire family, my younger brother Andy, my mother, Viola, and me, into our road-weary '49 Chevy and headed for Salinas. I discounted the ennui between my parents that morning as nothing particularly remarkable. There was always an abundance of entropy in our house.

My father prodded our tired old Chevy up California State Highway 152 toward the summit of Pacheco Pass. Andy bellyached about when we would finally get there. I tried my best to find every gray squirrel scurrying among the gnarled branches of the ancient live oaks that congregated like families along the sides of the attenuated, winding road through the Diablos. "There's another one," I'd shout. But no one expressed any interest.

The exhausted old Chevy expelled a sigh of relief as it crested the summit of the Pass and began to gather speed down its eastern slope.

"Can we stop at Bell Station, Daddy?" I'd slid forward onto the edge of the back seat with my chin resting on the back of my father's seat. The tang of Vitalis was strong in his thick, curly hair. I could feel the warmth of my father's body heat on my face, radiating off the leathery brown flesh at the back of his neck. And there was the familiar scent of his Gillette aftershave; a scent that would survive the landscape of fifty years and never fail to produce in me the image of my father's freshly shaved, smooth face.

"Got bidness in Salinas, boy," was his restive reply.

"On the way back, then?" My beseeching was met with edgy dissonance.

My father had slipped the old Chevy's helical, synchromesh three-speed transmission out of gear allowing the weighty Fisher body bolted onto its heavy-framed black chunk of Detroit steel to freewheel down the steep eastern grade. The perilous speed commanded his full concentration as the worm and roller steering system did its best to hold the car to the tight curves of the narrow two-lane road. Finally, standing both feet on the pedal of the old car's internal-expanding hydraulic drum brakes, he said, "We'll see," as the Chevy began to shimmy to a slower speed.

The smell of burnt asbestos hung heavy inside the car.

About two thirds of the way down

Pacheco Pass, we scooted past Bell Station. My father laid on the horn a good distance before and a long way past the roadside hamburger stand owned by Harold and Evelyn Ross. The old couple marched out to the side of the road and waved as our pitiably recognizable black Chevy jetted past them accelerating to nearly fifty miles per hour.

It would be three decades before I learned the tiny hamburger stand was not Bell Station Restaurant, which was located another three miles down the Pass on the north side of State Highway 152 and had existed since the 1800s. My father always said we were stopping at Bell Station, and that's what I understood and believed along with many other firm representations from my father when I was growing up. It was actually just old Harold Ross' makeshift hamburger stand: Harold's Five-For-a-Buck hamburgers. That inconsequential fact would not have tainted my inchoate affection for the magical place or its kind owners.

I turned and knelt in the back seat and waved back to the Rosses through the tapered oval rear window until the old couple's ephemeral image had shrunk to the size of two tiny dots. "I hope we get to stop on the way back."

"We'll see," my mother repeated. But that was little more than a pensive rumination. I'd heard that tone before.

Whenever my folks journeyed to Salinas, we always stayed with Edward and Irene Duncan. Edward Duncan and my father served together in the Army. The Duncans had a cherub-faced young son named Bubba, but Edward Duncan had called him Buggerman for so long, we all thought that was his real name; even Bubba thought so. He was about the same age as my mean-spirited, blue-eyed waif of a brother, Andy. The Duncans also had a daughter, Edna Chlodine, twelve-years-old. Edna Chlodine was two years older than me.

As much as I knew of the matter, I was in love with Edna Chlodine. I found it frustrating being drawn to an older woman, whom I only got to see and talk to on those infrequent occasions when my folks took the notion to drive over to Salinas for a Saturday night of hog butchering, beer drinking, and dancing to my mother's Cajun music thirty-three and a thirds on the rickety front porch of the Duncan's house.

The Duncans stood waiting for us out on that front porch which perilously clung to their tiny weathered farmhouse. My father drove towards them, up the long, rutted dirt road, which was hardly more than a well-worn tractor path between fifty acres of ripening tomatoes on the north and seventy-five acres of pungent maturing garlic to the south. That day Edna Chlodine wore a sky blue taffeta dress with lace around the hem and a large bow at the collar instead of the overalls she frequently favored. Even from a distance I could see her jet-black curls toppling profusely onto her shoulders in

stark contrast to her alabaster skin. Bugga'
had a Parcheesi board under one arm and a
Yahtzee game under the other. The games
were a treat for Andy and me because no
such waste of good money was permitted in
our house.

Edward Duncan and my father were
both slight-framed, wiry young men of no
more than a hundred sixty-five pounds. The
usual convivial greeting between my father
and Edward Duncan—a few awkward
crouching boxing punches thrown while
hopping about like a couple of monkeys
followed by a big hug, and then Edward
Duncan strutting over to get a cold Lucky
Lager and imperiously pressing it into my
father's hand—did not take place that day. I
found it hard to understand how they could
fight against the Nazis or Japanese and win
any war, but they had. My mother and Irene
Duncan somberly busied themselves
unloading our old Chevy. I was only
vaguely aware of the hushed conversation
taking place between Edward Duncan and

my father.

Suddenly, a warm, soft hand slipped into mine, eliminating any interest I had in the mysteriously grim adults. I jumped at the feel of the fluffy-down smoothness of her tiny palm. When Edna Chlodine touched my hand, it was as if I was being burned but could not remove my fingers from the flame.

"Want to play Parcheesi, Cotton?" Edna Chlodine's sloe eyes possessed the grave intensity of cooled obsidian. "Just you and me," she whispered, a provocative half-grin edging her pouty lips with promise. I permitted her to pull me away by the hand. Andy and Bugga' had the Yahtzee board out with dice and game pieces spread about the scuffed linoleum floor of the crowded living room.

The next morning, Edward Duncan and my father were up early and gone before us kids had our breakfast. Irene and my mother still seemed unusually subdued.

"You kids get cleaned up ... go on out

`n play so's me'n Viola can straighten this kitchen." Irene Duncan wiped pancake batter from her hands onto her stained, apron.

We all scrambled for the sink in the one-bathroom house. I had to restrain Andy and Bugga' so Edna Chlodine could go first. She bent from the waist, hands on her hips and jutted her chin out toward our brothers when she pranced past them into the bathroom. She held the door ajar slightly once she was inside and smiled at me for several moments.

"Hurry up," Bugga' yelled.

"Shush your mouth and wait your turn, Buggerman Duncan," his mother ordered.

Edward Duncan was a foreman for La Casita Farms in the Salinas Valley. They held thousands of acres under cultivation and grew just about everything: garlic, onions, lettuce, carrots and tomatoes. They even had large fruit orchards. Edward

Duncan always sent my father back home to the San Joaquin Valley with a surfeit of vegetables and fruit that would last two weeks or more. Sometimes we couldn't eat everything before some of it went bad.

La Casita supplied Edward Duncan with a dilapidated, but cozy little house near the processing sheds, which sat apart from the Mexican field hands who lived in the tarpaper shacks out along the farthest back edges of the fields against the Santa Lucias. The outside walls of Edward Duncan's boxy little house were clapboard that had been burnished gray from weather and age and the absence of any paint. At least the roof didn't leak the way ours would when it rained. There were only four tiny rooms inside the house, separated by paper-thin walls of pealing plaster and tragic wallpaper. But it was a castle compared to what the Mexicans lived in.

Edna Chlodine and Buggerman were forced to abandon their room for my father and mother. Irene made a pallet on the floor

in her room for Edna Chlodine, and we three
boys were put up on the couch that broke
down the middle to form a bed in the living
room.

Before turning in at night, regardless
of the weather or time of year, Edward
Duncan, my father, Buggerman, Andy and I
would march out behind the house and line
up facing the tall row of eucalyptus trees
that were there to provide a break from the
fierce winds, which frequently ventured in
off the Pacific Ocean lying near to the west,
just beyond the peaks of the Santa Lucias,
which run south from Monterey along the
entire western edge of the Salinas Valley
and undulate downward like the slope of one
gentle-giant of a volcano toward the
outermost limits of the thousands of acres of
crops spreading out before us—and piss. It
was an act I considered heroic on some
occasions, wind whipped urine not being a
thing that is easily controlled except to make
damn sure you kept it downwind.

There could be a lot of laughter over

the farting and ribald remarks that went on before everyone fell asleep. Edward Duncan was famous for farting very loud, then yelling, in an insouciant kind of way, rebuking and berating my father for the vile indiscretion. "You better get up and clean yourself, Percy," he'd yell.

My father could be depended on to counter Edward's insults with, "You better see what's a runnin' down back o' your leg, Edward Duncan!"

Irene and Edna Chlodine were clearly mortified by such uncouth behavior, but my own mother was known to contribute to the crudeness on occasion, followed by an insincere, "Well, excuse me!" which might have been acceptable were she not to continue the act several more times.

The packing sheds located near the house offered the perfect place to play, free from adult meddling. That day Buggerman led the way to the edge of a field behind one of the long sheds where, though none of us were hungry, we all gorged ourselves on vine-ripened tomatoes before it occurred to Andy to start throwing the rotten ones against the wall.

Edna Chlodine charmed me into the idea of eluding our brothers. She grabbed my hand, and the two of us raced off down the side of the long, low-lying shed just as it occurred to Andy and Bugga' that we'd make more interesting targets for their rotten projectiles than the static sidewalls of the shed. But Edna Chlodine knew her way and pulled me, ducking in between two buildings, down a narrow passageway and across a set of wide rutted tire tracks to a second row of buildings. She turned again and darted to one she knew and slid the heavy corniced door open just enough for the two of us to squeeze inside. I helped her slide the door closed and we waited, panting, our faces pressed tight against the grave smooth planks in the subdued light of the cavernous space to hear if our brothers had seen us.

It was cool and mysteriously quiet inside the darkened shed. Bright rays of sunlight sliced through the cracks in the walls like knife blades and illuminated millions of tiny floating dust motes in the air, creating a vast universe of shiny suspended particles like stars in an indigo night.

Outside, Andy and Bugga' searched and guessed at which door we'd disappeared into. But there were dozens of doors we might have slipped behind down the long corridor of buildings facing each other. "I'm gonna' smash this rotten one right in Edna Chlodine's hair," threatened a giggling Buggerman.

Edna Chlodine giggled silently. She held her fingers to her lips and gripped my hand as if it were a prize from a carnival. It was exciting, the waiting and listening to the voices of our brothers receding. They'd turned and run the wrong way.

We relaxed then and began to move

cautiously about in the half-light of the capacious shed. It was a long low building used for sorting fresh picked crops before they were bundled up and sent to markets or packing companies. Rows and rows of empty wide slatted bushel baskets were stacked against the inside walls. At the far end of the building was a small office where tallies were kept—Edward Duncan's command post from which he kept a vigilant eye over his *lazy* Mexican field hands. Edna Chlodine had obviously been there before.

"Come on," she urged, tugging at my arm. "There's a loft above Daddy's office where we can hide."

The space was wide but not high enough for us to stand up straight. Its floor rested directly above the doorway into Edward Duncan's office. The loft was used to store straw mats for drying fruit, and when we crawled across them, I caught sweet fragrances of fermented pear and apricot. Edna Chlodine led me all the way to the back of the loft where we finally collapsed backward onto our knees facing each other. We sat there while an awkward silence gathered between us. A bright ray of sunlight cut diagonally across Edna Chlodine's face and made her look like an Indian with war paint.

"You wanna hold hands some more?" Edna Chlodine coached me.

I fidgeted. "Sure, I guess so." I let her take my hand once more. There was that sensation of impossible softness again when she ran her thumb gently back and forth over the top of my little finger. My entire being ignited in a hot, crawling slow-burning stir that began in a place inside me I didn't understand.

My eyes slowly adjusted to the dim light. I gawked furtively about our aromatic hiding place having not the slightest clue as to what I should do next. With my free hand, I briskly scratched the top of my closely shaved head. I could not suppress a dumb grin each time I made eye contact with Edna

Chlodine, whose gaze seemed locked on me like the crosshairs in a riflescope. I could feel my dimples cutting deep into my cheeks. Then my eyes would dart away to some new object only to return to meet her intense gaze once more, which I always found leveled unflinchingly on me. I remember wishing I had the confidence to do that. I did remember to make sure to display my teeth when I smiled. Everybody talked about how perfect my teeth were. I knew they were one of my best features. I was, however, self-conscious about my ears, which stuck out severely and were made to look much worse for the moment by the hideous head-shave my father had given Andy and me, owing to the fact we'd gotten a dose of ringworm from a litter of wild kittens we'd found. And it is true that I was quite skinny. But I had better teeth than just about anybody. At least I was as tall as she, which I knew was important to Edna Chlodine.

That morning she'd abandoned her

taffeta dress in favor of the overalls she preferred most of the time. She wore a long-sleeved yellow-green shirt under the shoulder straps and bib of her baggy pants that opened wide down the sides all the way to her petite waist. Edna Chlodine was not as skinny as I was. She was slender and pretty much straight up and down except for the new lumps beginning to protrude outward from her chest. She bore a magnificent mop of black ringlets that swirled about her face. The density of her dark eyes was such that there appeared to be no pupil in the middle, just these two intense black opals in a sea of large, round white orbs outlined by very long, thick eyelashes. Her brows were heavy and dark, too, but not comical or unfortunate; they were inspiring. She had this way of raising one brow, cocking her head, ropes of heavy black curls floating to that side and down her shoulder—and smiling at me. Her hair was so shiny black sometimes in the sun it glistened blue.

"You know how to kiss, Cotton?"

"Only girl I ever kissed is momma," I admitted.

"Wanna learn?" she whispered, bending forward toward me, smiling, pleading it seemed.

Even at the age of twelve her tiny voice sounded naughty to me. Her heavy long curls hung evenly along the sides of her face from a deep part down the middle of her head. There were tiny beads of moisture just above the turn of her upper lip, under her dainty nose. She inclined her face downward focusing on my hands in hers, and then looked out at me through the tops of her eyes, through that massive mop-tunnel of black.

"How is it you know how?" I wanted to know, feeling jealous.

"Been practicing on the back of my wrist," she explained without regard for my tone. "Here ... watch." Edna Chlodine lifted her hand toward her mouth and let the palm fall backward exposing the soft white flesh of the underside of her wrist. To this day, I have never experienced any greater intensity of response to a sensuous act than I felt at that moment watching Edna Chlodine. She licked her lips and pressed them softly against the pure white flesh of her exposed wrist. I watched her, hypnotically entranced and strangely aroused by her demonstration for reasons I could not as yet understand.

"Now, you try it," she insisted.

I was unsure—self-conscious. "I don't think boys do that kind of stuff," I objected, adjusting the weight on my legs, which were beginning to tingle from loss of blood flow.

"It's easy," argued Edna Chlodine. "Look." She seized my right hand, pulled it toward her, rolled my arm over to expose the underside of my wrist and lifted it close to her mouth. She stopped briefly, flicked her tongue across her lips once more while gazing into my eyes, and then she pressed her soft, moist lips onto my wrist.

An out-of-control brush fire burned its way up my spine and attacked my brain. I sucked in my breath with a sharp gasp.

Edna Chlodine dropped my hand immediately. "What's wrong?" she wanted to know, furrows screwing across her forehead like a row plow across a fresh-raked field.

"No ... nothing," I whispered, too embarrassed to speak. For several seconds I rubbed my wrist where she'd kissed it and stared down at my knees. Finally I asked her, "Is it gonna feel like that on my mouth?"

"I don't know," admitted Edna Chlodine. Her answer made me feel special.

Silent anticipation went on until Edna Chlodine raised herself up onto her knees in front of me and whispered again. "Let's try it, Cotton." My nose was only inches from where I knew her bellybutton was.

I hesitated but followed her lead. On my knees, I found my face only inches away from hers. I could feel her chest heaving, and I smelled her sweet, warm breath still tinged with the scent of fresh tomato. My own chest was heaving so hard I was certain she must have been able to hear it. In that moment, I thought Edna Chlodine was surely the most beautiful girl on the face of the earth. She licked her lips again, and they became sparkly in the streak of light that coursed across her face. I licked my lips and hoped I didn't look silly. Edna Chlodine took both of my hands in hers, closed her eyes and tilted her head back a little so that her lips made an easy target.

Suddenly, a light came on in Edward Duncan's office, and at once a deluge of sound, mean and discordant, shattered the possibility of our moment. We heard our fathers' voices. We froze into a pair of statues; our hearts hammering like war drums for a whole new reason.

"Damn, Edward," I heard my father

yell, "I cain't believe you in charge of a great big ole outfit like this here `n they's no way you can use a good man like me."

"Look here, Percy Maenus," we heard Edward say in his defense, "you a mechanic, not a farmhand."

"Hell, I know that, Edward," my father argued. "But you got all them lazy-ass wetbacks to keep an eye on. They jest like them niggers back home. Cain't turn ye back on `em—shuck off ever time." I knew my father's only real experience with any Mexican was working side-by-side with them picking apricots near Fresno, and not one of those Mexicans could have been called lazy-assed.

"Percy," Edward Duncan countered, "I'm mighty sorry you lost your job."

Suddenly, I understood everything. I saw now why the trip had come up so unexpectedly and why the grownups were doing so much whispering around the others and me.

What moments before had been a cocoon of mysterious promise became a prison of claustrophobic bleakness.

"But I cain't jest hire you on to watch over them Mesikens."

"You mean you afraid to," my father sneered. "Never thought I'd see the day Edward Duncan turn chicken shit!" My father spit the words out as though he was goading a coward, but Edward Duncan was no coward, nor would he yield to my father's profligacy.

"I mean, I cain't, Percy. Out here it don't work like back home."

The conviction in Edward Duncan's voice was growing. My full attention had turned from Edna Chlodine to the argument that was raging just inches beneath where we remained hidden

Edward Duncan pressed on. "Percy, you a good mechanic. Best they is. 'N you got you a place to live over yonder in the

Valley. People knows you. Hell, you only been out o' work one day. Word gets out you lookin'—"

My father cut him off. "Kiss my ass, Edward Duncan," he spewed. "Why don't you jest come right out `n say what you mean to say? I ain't good enough to work over here with y'all."

At that point I really wondered if Edward Duncan might not thump my father right in the nose for cussing at him like that. They'd gotten into fistfights before when they were drunk.

Edna Chlodine and I flinched when one of them slammed his fist down hard on something metal. "Percy Maenus, that's pure-d-bullshit!" Edward Duncan pronounced each syllable of the cuss words deliberately. "I been knowin' you near on to ten year now `n you know damn well that jest ain't so."

All of a sudden it was deadly silent.

Edna Chlodine and I were paralyzed with fear, afraid to breathe. I could make out the slow shuffling of feet like someone pacing back and forth. One of them stopped in the doorway just below the loft. Whoever it was might have squinted into the darkness of the shed before my father whined, "I thought you was my friend, Edward Duncan. Thought you might hep me move up in life a little."

"I am your friend, Percy. But—"

My father wouldn't allow Edward Duncan to continue. "I'll be loadin' up Viola and the boys … headin' back."

"But y'all jest got here."

I could hear the manqué in Edward Duncan's words.

My father ignored him and opened the door. "Best get back `n try to find me a job `fore my kids goes hungry—not that you could give a shit."

One of them stomped out of the tally

room.

A few moments later the light was flipped off, and Edward Duncan could be heard shouting after my father to hold up and wait for him.

I heard the key turn in the lock and waited several moments before getting up. Edna Chlodine tried to pull me back down onto my knees, but I shook free from her grip. I was so ashamed I couldn't bear to face her. I wasn't sure I could ever look into her eyes again. "We gotta' get back up to the house," I insisted. I wanted to get out of kissing Edna Chlodine right then about as badly as I'd wanted to go through with the act just minutes before. I felt sick, and worse than that—inferior.

Edna Chlodine didn't say anything more. Her head bowed; she reluctantly followed me out the same way we'd come in.

By the time we'd trudged back up to the house, my mother was on her way out the front door, tears streaking her face and a bag of clothes in her arms. "Gather up your stuff and get in the car," she ordered, without stopping to explain.

Irene Duncan was following her. More like, chasing her, actually. "Y'all come on `n stay the weekend, Vi. Things'll seem so much better Sunday afternoon."

But my mother didn't get a chance to answer. It wouldn't have mattered. My father had his mind made up. He appeared in the doorway dragging Andy by the arm. Between them they had the rest of our belongings, which really wasn't much. "Get in the car, boy," he ordered as he brushed past Edna Chlodine and me. "We headin' home."

In a matter of minutes we were loaded into the old Chevy and with none of the ceremony associated with our arrival, tore off in the direction of the main highway, spinning the tires, kicking up dust and gravel as we went.

I knelt in the back seat wanting very much to wave to Edna Chlodine, but I could not. She looked so unhappy. Instinct told me I'd made a big mistake not kissing her when I had the chance. She quickly disappeared in the dust clouds like a dream. She was gone by the time the wheels of our old Chevy hit the pavement of the highway and the dust had cleared.

It was almost noon when my father made the transition off of Highway 101 back onto State Highway 152. My mother slunk as close to the passenger door as she could get and stared out her window in silence. My father drove with his window down smoking one cigarette after another, tossing the glowing butts out of the speeding vehicle.

The '49 Chevy slowed from strain as it began winding its way back up the long eastern slope of Pacheco Pass. I was surprised when my father whipped the car off the road next to the little wooden building beside the creek at Bell Station—

our Bell Station.

Harold and Evelyn didn't seem to be around. The only sound was the eerie tranquil silence one encounters in remote places, interrupted by the popping of hot metal under the hood of the car as it began to cool. Then there was a gentle soughing of a light breeze playing in the upper branches of the giant oaks. I could just make out the occasional gurgling sounds of water tumbling over stones.

"Anybody, 'round?" yelled my father, fracturing the peaceful quiet without the slightest appreciation for it.

"Out here," came a voice from the outhouse across the shallow creek. "Wondered if you'd stop on your way back." Harold Ross hobbled on his one good leg up the side hill toward us.

"How ya'll been, Harold?" my father inquired. "Got a cold one for a buddy?" he wheedled.

Harold hesitated. He'd told my father on many occasions he didn't like selling beer to his customers. Had no license to sell the stuff. Mean lots of trouble if he got caught.

"Gimme a six pack o' Lucky Lager, Harold. Anybody stops, I brought it with me." My father reached through the open driver's window of the Chevy, pulled out an opener and offed a bottle cap on the front fender. Then he guzzled half the bottle in one hit.

"Fix the family something to eat?" Harold offered. I could see that the squat gray-haired old man sensed trouble and was proceeding cautiously. Our family'd been stopping at his place for a few years. Harold had experienced many faces of my father. When he was happy, in a good mood, there was no better man to be around than my father, Percy Maenus. But he could be as foul a character as there ever was if he felt crossways to the world. Harold understood to beware.

"How 'bout them five-fer-a-buck hamburgers o' yours?" My father tilted back his head and chugged the rest of his bottle of beer. He threw the dead soldier to the side of the road.

Harold shook his head and went around the side of his ramshackle setup to the door. He could pick up the bottle later. No point in running the risk of pissing my father off. His kitchen was a tiny one-room, thin plywood affair that had begun to separate around all of its edges from exposure to rain and sun. A front flap yawned upward like a circus clown's mouth and formed a partial shade awning when the sun was at its zenith.

Four rickety, leaf-cluttered picnic tables were spread haplessly about under the branches of the oak trees. Lichens and moss grew on the fusty two-by-sixes where they were in constant shade. My father pointed to his favorite table, brushed away a few leaves and put the remainder of his six-pack on it. "You want one, Vi?" he offered, opening another Lucky Lager.

My mother didn't drink, and she didn't approve of my father's drinking, either. It was his way of letting her know he didn't give a shit; his way of warning her she'd better keep her mouth shut. My mother was five-two standing on a box and couldn't have topped out at more than ninety-five pounds. When I think of her now, I know she was an attractive woman. She had dark, wavy hair past her shoulders and always wore her lips painted bright red and spoke what little English she knew with a lilting Cajun twang. When she smiled, her dark brown eyes crinkled behind her glasses, and the same dimples she had given me cut deep into her soft, flushed cheeks. Though I never knew my father to ever raise his hand to her, he'd posture as though he might. My mother glared back at him.

Out of the bowels of Harold's hut came the sound of a banging pan. "How ya'll been?" Harold shouted while he set up to cook.

"Not worth a shit," my father yelled. "Lost my gotdamn job!"

I decided to take a chance at getting away before he downed another beer and turned ugly. "Daddy, me `n Andy go play by the creek?"

"Keep your asses where I kin see ye, boy. We gonna' get back on the road soon as we eat. Ye hear me?" Eating was a euphemism for when he'd finished his six-pack of beer.

"Yes, sir," I shouted over my shoulder as Andy and I tore off running. I stayed close enough to remain within earshot of the conversation being shouted back and forth between Harold Ross and my father.

Harold cut in. "Sorry to hear that. Anything lined up?"

My father stared across the top of his beer bottle at my mother while he downed another half bottle in one swig. "Thought I had somethin' over in Salinas. Didn't pan out," he said, glaring at my mother as if Edward Duncan refusing to hire him was somehow her fault.

Everything that went wrong in my father's life carried with it a façade of blame for the predicate; if it wasn't my mother's fault, then it was Andy's or mine.

"Hey, Percy," Harold shouted over the clanging of a metal spatula. "You know Al Benson, don't you? Runs the service department at Kaljan's Chevrolet over to Newman?"

My father was busy opening another bottle of beer. "Know of `im," he claimed, glancing up at my mother, "don't know `im personal." This was unusual because my father swore he knew everybody 'personal', including Ike. He went on to finish his third Lucky Lager.

Harold stopped and stuck his head out over the counter. "He's looking for a mechanic."

My father came rigid for a moment, stared briefly at my mother. "How is it you come to know of it?"

"Sister lives over to Hollister." Harold's voice was muffled, but I could make out what was being said. "Stopped by here last Sunday on his way home from seeing her. Says he's having a helluva time finding somebody. I'd go see 'im, I was you."

The mid-afternoon air had begun to cool and was growing heavy. The smoke from Harold's wood-fired grill hung heavy in the low branches of the trees. The small clearing, all the way down along the creek, had become redolent with the smell of burning hamburger grease. My stomach growled while I squatted over the rocks in the shallow creek. I was only half listening to the conversation by then having been distracted by the serious search for gold.

"Maybe I'll do that," my father replied. "Maybe I'll do that when we get back this afternoon." Hope, if not optimism, had found its way into my father's voice. He was like that, my father. He could find frisson in the slightest of possibilities. He just never seemed to have many.

"Why not," Harold said over his shoulder. "Got nothin' to lose." He turned and placed two hamburgers on the counter. "Couple o' hot ones here if somebody wants to get started."

My father took both of them and began to eat.

I came running up to the table. "Look what I caught." I held up the fragile, pink creature in the palm of my hand for everyone to see.

"Salamander," Harold Ross announced from his kitchen. "Lots of `em around this time o' year."

My mother hated all things slimy. "You keep that thing away from me, Cotton Maenus." My mother squealed. Disgust drifted over her face like a gathering storm, and her hands drew up under her chin. She squirmed uneasily, reeling backward.

My father didn't bother to look up. Grease oozed from the corners of his mouth. He grumbled, "Get shed o' that damn thang, boy. Get warts in ye hands carryin' it `round."

Harold Ross came to my defense. "Percy, that's just a tale. Salamander won't hurt the boy."

My father chewed noisily, raised his head slowly and fixed his threatening glower on Harold Ross for his indiscretion. "I said ... get shed of it, boy."

I retreated immediately.

A few minutes later Harold announced the other three hamburgers were ready. My mother and Andy and I ate alone while my father and Harold walked down by the water and talked.

Bell Station was my favorite place of

all on Pacheco Pass and Harold Ross one of
my favorite people. When my father was in
a good mood, we would sometimes stay an
entire afternoon, my father drinking beer
and eating peanuts. My mother and Evelyn
Ross would sit quietly at a separate table and
crochet doilies while Harold held Andy and
me captive with fanciful tales about lover's
leap high up in Pacheco Pass; how, long ago
a young Indian warrior from one tribe and a
beautiful Indian princess from another had
climbed all the way to the top of the leap
one day and threw themselves off together
because their two rival tribes had forbidden
them to love each other. Harold swore that
their spirits still roamed the canyons around
those parts, and when the wind was moaning
high in the trees, if you listened closely, you
could hear their voices calling to each other.
I flashed on Edna Chlodine looking so much
like a beautiful Indian princess up in the loft
that day. I wondered if we would ever be in
love like that. I already knew I was in love. I
wasn't so sure about throwing myself off of
lover's leap over it though.

By the time we finished eating, my father was anxious to get moving again. We all washed quickly down at the creek and soon were back on the road.

The tension between my parents seemed greatly reduced, and they spoke quietly in the front seat about the job opening at Kaljan's Chevrolet. It was a good outfit, my father held. He'd heard of this Benson fellow. He was said to be a good man to work for. My mother knew a woman who worked for their family. Maybe … maybe things would work out for them. But Edward Duncan was still an asshole according to my father. And I knew from that conviction it was going to be a good while before I would see Edna Chlodine again. The conversation and supposing continued in the front seat while my father pushed the old Chevy hard up over Pacheco Pass.

Convinced my parents were completely preoccupied and Andy was fast asleep, I reached into my shirt pocket and

found the tiny curled up salamander. I pulled
the gentle amphibian out and held it gingerly
in my palm. Its bulbous pink toes curled
over the edge of my forefinger and felt
sticky. When it attempted to crawl away, I
closed my hand lightly around it, allowing
only its front feet and head to rest along the
leading edge of my index finger. I held it
close to my face and studied its large bugged
out eyes. I deliberated over the detail of its
feet, which were formed like tiny, perfectly
defined prenatal hands. I observed that its
delicate, pink body was mottled with white
polka dots. Edna Chlodine had a dress
something like that. While I stared at the
fragile, anthropomorphic creature's mouth, I
found myself thinking about Edna
Chlodine's warm moist lips once more; how
I'd come so close to pressing my lips onto
hers. I wondered how long it might be
before my father would forgive Edward
Duncan and I'd get another chance. I
thought about how it felt when she kissed
my wrist and the wild sensations coursing
all through my body. It was scary, but I

wanted to try it again. I definitely intended trying it. Next time … next time … I'd kiss her right on the lips.

*   *   *

They're all gone now. Buggerman was the first to slip away while he was still young. He was in his second year of junior college in Watsonville. He was driving home for the weekend one foggy Friday night. A drunk driver veered across the middle of a two-lane road, and they crashed head on. Bubba was killed instantly.

Irene Duncan was never quite the same after that.

Several years later Edward Duncan dropped dead in an onion field one day from a heart attack.

My little brother, Andy, was stabbed to death in prison in 1978. He was serving two life sentences in the Louisiana State Penitentiary for murder. Percy and Viola Maenus, my father and mother, never recovered from that nightmare and unmercifully committed slow suicide at the hands of Phillip Morris. They smoked themselves into an early grave a mere seven weeks apart in February some years ago, just as winter had claimed the last of the leaves of all the fruit trees in their beautiful garden.

Irene Duncan was there to help me say good-bye to them and then died herself a year later, in her sleep. Maybe she'd just grown weary of what life had dealt her.

Edna Chlodine and I never again saw the opportunity to find our way back to the promise of that first innocent kiss. She died more than twenty years ago when she was forty-three-years-old; brutally beaten to death by an abusive alcoholic husband she just could not bring herself to walk away from.

Me—I frequently find myself still hoping and believing—tenderness must exist somewhere.

END

If you enjoyed the stories of: A Salamander at Bell Station … and other tales … Beyond East of Eden, please take a moment to go to Amazon and place a review of this book.

Other works by R.P. McCabe include:

Betrayed - published 2012

Thick Fog in Pacheco Pass - published 2013

Slaughtered is Mr. McCabe's current writing project. The novel is Vol. 2 in his Charlie Caldwell Crime Series currently scheduled for release in 2015.

Mr. McCabe enjoys hearing from his readers.

http://www.novelistrpmccabe.com